5/17

Winnie,

Blessings to you!
Congrats on winning, &
thank you for reading
Inspy Romance!

Julie Arduini

Entangled:
Surrendering the Past

Julie Arduini

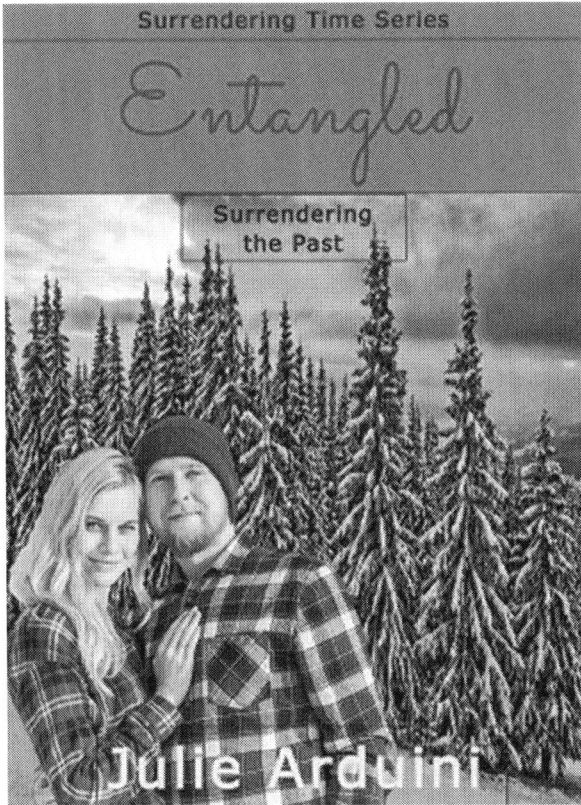

The Surrendering Time Series

Dedication:

To anyone who thinks their choices are too awful or too late to live in forgiveness, you are deeply loved and highly valued. This book is dedicated to you.

Chapter One

A twenty-minute run. That's all I need. Just enough time to feel free.

Instead, the Hamilton County DA places a neon green gift bag in my hand. He then looks to the crowd. "Just forty-eight hours and our very own Carla Rowling will go from handcuffs to haircuts."

The Piseco Inn meeting room is wall-to-wall people. My fellow law enforcement, paramedic, and fire and rescue colleagues hand me gifts and joke at the idea of me leaving for beauty school.

I paste on a smile as I lift a pair of black running shoes with hot pink trim from layers of tissue paper, but my focus is on my breathing. Steady and even. Like when I'm running.

"From squad car to standing all day. What a switch." Fred Beebe, retired bank president, grins.

I stand and balance my arm on Joanie, the county dispatcher, as I slip off the three-inch heels I borrowed from my best friend Jenna and try on the comfy shoes.

"Hey, Carla! Will you wear those as you run with scissors to chase perps out of your hair salon?" Jack Hunt, my replacement, snorts from laughing too hard.

"Do they fit?" Joanie looks to the empty box on the floor where wrapping paper and ribbon litter the area.

I nod, let go, and sit. "They're so comfortable I'm going to wear them for the rest of my party." And as soon as I can, break these sneakers in. There's nothing like the feel of new running shoes, and no better time to use them than when the walls feel like they're closing in.

Will Marshall, my truck-driving boyfriend of less than a year, adjusts his bright orange hunting cap and places his hand over mine. "Carla, those shoes are going to be great for the long days at your salon." He turns to Joanie and winks. "What a nice gift. You all have the best ideas to transform our favorite sheriff to our new stylist."

Looking around, I see my former colleagues from around Hamilton, the only county in New York State that doesn't have traffic lights. The people smile and chant my name. Their grins seem sincere as they point to the table full of packages. Gifts I'll never deserve.

"C'mon, keep opening your presents so we can have cake." My thirteen-year old son, Noah, never wastes time, especially when it comes to food. He walks over and grabs a stack of wrapped boxes

I sigh and rest my moist hands on my lap. "Okay. Hand me another. By the looks of that pile, we'll be here all week."

Will chuckles. "Sweetie, you don't have that kind of time. You start beauty school in two days."

I glance at the door, my breathing no longer steady, but fast. Beads of sweat form at my hairline and I regret not putting my hair in a ponytail without bangs. Probably everyone's counting the perspiration drops falling on my jeans.

I *have* to run.

⧗⧗⧗

Thirty minutes later, Judge Franklin cuts the half-vanilla, half-chocolate cake. The confection features black and white iced decorations of free-hand scissors and hair dryers. My best friend, Jenna Anderson, starts passing out pieces. Everyone's so busy chatting and eating they don't notice my escape.

God, forgive me for leaving my party. I glance around the perimeter of the conference room and tiptoe to the rear door. After my smooth exit, I leave the full parking lot and head for Old Piseco Road. "This is too fast, Lord, all of it. Inheriting all that money from Howard Wheaton. Starting beauty school. Jenna and Ben Regan getting married. Noah being a teenager." I pick up the pace. "Will and me."

I'm half a mile down the road when it hits. It's January. Although there isn't snow on the road, it isn't warm out. My red sweater and casual jeans are for indoor fun. Leaving the party—not my best idea.

"I can't shake the fear, God. I'm not worthy. I'll never measure up. Just like being sheriff, it'll be the same as a stylist. Those people

10

belong. I never will. I'll always be the girl who got pregnant in high school."

I turn and head back to the Piseco Inn, using each step to squash my fears about all the kindness I don't deserve behind me. With a quarter-mile left to go, I hear gravel crack under moving tires.

"Carla? Is that you?"

I pause, folding my hands against my chest.

The vehicle stops. The health center SUV.

Please don't let Wayne be inside.

"Rowling, what are you doing away from your party?" Paramedic Nathan McCoy leans out the driver window. "You don't even have a coat on. C'mon, get in. What's gotten into you, anyway?"

The passenger door opens, and Wayne Peterson, my high school sweetheart and Noah's dad, slides over. "Carla's doing what she does best. She loves to run."

I roll my eyes. "Well, you're definitely the one who inspired me to start."

⏳⏳⏳

I didn't think I was gone long, but when we pull up at the inn entrance five minutes later, Will has his coat on and walks toward the lot.

"Okay, Nate. Drop me off here. Thanks." I reach for the handle.

"Your boyfriend's looking for you. Do you think you made Will, the great hunter of the Adirondacks, mad?" Wayne's silky voice has a chuckle at the end.

I close my eyes and take a deep breath. "If you two are coming to my party, don't forget to put my gifts on the table." As soon as the vehicle stops, I slide out and jog to the line of cars without looking back. "Will. Over here." I wave my hands.

Will returns my wave and smiles, jogging toward me. "There you are. Where've you been? Jenna joked that maybe you saw the cake was half vanilla and you left."

That Jenna. We both love our chocolate.

I meet Will in the center of the parking lot and shake my head. "No, I just needed a little air."

11

Not even the vast mountains of Upstate New York can give me enough space.

Will takes the crook of my arm. Our steps are slow back to the celebration. "You were gone quite a while." His deep voice isn't much more than a whisper.

I lean into him, partly for warmth. "Was I? Well, I wanted to test the shoes."

He arches his eyebrows. "Without your workout clothes?"

My voice rises an octave. "It wasn't a full run. Like I said, just checking them out."

Will pushes the main door and we walk through. The conference room still has laughter and voices echoing past the lobby. "Okay. So, are they everything you thought they'd be?"

I blink, thinking back to the nice pace I had going before I realized I was cold. The pounding of shoes on the road, and only that noise of refuge the outdoors brings.

"If I'd had a jacket on, I'd probably still be running." I grin.

Will gives my arm a squeeze. "Oh, Carla. You and your jogs. I think that's a form of therapy for you, although I'm not quite sure what you run for. Or maybe it's running from something." He scratches his goatee.

Before I can reply, I realize Will's right. Except I'm most likely running from someone. Because as soon as I see Wayne and Nathan enter the party, I freeze.

Wayne's suddenly ahead of us, pouring a glass of punch. For a second I'm transported back to prom, when his punch spilled on my dress. His touch so soft.

A chill brings me back to present time.

"Carla? Did you hear me?" Will's grip on my arm is now a squeeze.

I shake my head and glance over to Will.

Stay in the present, girl.

"I asked if it was good." Will's voice is as soft and tender as his personality.

"I'm not sure I understand. What?"

Will scratches his goatee. "Honey, are you tired? The party. Are you having a good time?" He lets go of my arm.

I take in a deep breath and wipe my forehead. The tremors in my hand return.

Wayne walks by and raises his punch in my direction, like a mock salute.

I clear my throat and turn my attention to my boyfriend. "Yes. Sorry, Will. I think the sneakers are perfect. So much so I'll get a second pair for work and use these strictly for running."

Will looks at me funny, his eyebrows raised, but says nothing.

Noah spots his dad and in three strides, is at his side. Wayne gives him a high-five, the drink spilling a little onto the floor. The two laugh, and whether my first boyfriend remembers our many junior year high school memories or not, he turns to me and winks.

With a sigh I look down at my new shoes. "And I plan lots and lots of running."

⧗⧗⧗

Two hours later, Will turns off the ignition and pats my knee. "I've got an early delivery tomorrow, but if you show me where you want all your gifts, I can help Noah unload them."

I dig into my purse for the house keys. "I didn't think about where I wanted everything. Honestly, I thought it was just an 'eat cake and wish me well' kind of party. I didn't expect presents." I open the passenger door and slide out.

Will leaves the driver's seat and walks to the truck cab, tugging at the cover snaps whistling some song I can't figure out. "Why? Everyone loves you. The whole village is excited about your dream coming true." The song continues.

Once he lifts the cover, we reach in for gift bags containing hair dryers, scissors, combs, razors, and gift cards. As we bring the loot to the front porch, I balance bags with my keys and work on opening the door.

Noah chuckles. "Yeah, Mom. Brian's mom said she wants you to color the white out of her hair."

13

Images of women needing perms, color jobs, and haircuts flash through my mind. *Lord, help me do well.*

"Sweetheart? Where do you want everything?" Will's green eyes pierce mine.

"The spare room."

Noah leads us down the hallway, turning the light on with his elbow. Will glances down the hall toward my room. "Have you packed yet?"

I pause. Don't I still have two days? "No. Remember, I had a party? I've been kind of busy." My smile is as weak as my answer.

"But you're going to be away during the week. You'll need a few things, right?" Will walks into the spare room and places the bags on the carpet.

I unload my new belongings on the rug, too. "I'm going to Gloversville for school, not Georgia. I'm staying with a widow who has a house. Her kitchen and bathroom is stocked."

Noah drops the contents next to mine, then glances at each of us as we talk.

"But you need clothes. Supplies for school." If Will scratches that goatee one more time, I'm going to shave it.

"I have time. It's not that big of a deal." At least if I avoid thinking about it.

Since no one moves, I start for the living room.

Will follows. "Okay, it's just that this is an exciting time for you. Your schooling and licensing fees are paid in full. There's enough money left for you to purchase a shop. These gifts fell in your lap, and you don't seem that excited. If my schooling and licenses had been paid in advance, I would have packed the hour I heard Howard Wheaton left that money."

Will Marshall deserves such a gift. Lifetime Speculator Falls resident. Would give the shirt off his back to anyone. Wouldn't hurt anyone. Why he's with me keeps me up most nights. When I'm not thinking about why Howard would ever leave someone like me that kind of money.

I try to sound nonchalant. "I had to tackle things by priority. Give my notice at the sheriff's office. Make sure Wayne was okay with you overseeing everything with Noah during the week. I'll pack tomorrow." Or minutes before I have to leave for Gloversville.

He sighs and adjusts the neon orange hat that rarely leaves his head. "Fine. I don't want to fight with you. I was making an observation. I thought maybe you weren't really into this change. That maybe you were having second thoughts." He leans over and gives me a quick kiss before leaving.

Noah saunters into the kitchen and opens the fridge, while I stand in place. Second thoughts? Try third and fourth.

Chapter Two

It's entertaining to watch Noah scramble down the hall as soon as I call out, "Bacon's ready." The black waves in his hair bounce as he slides past me on our wooden floor.

"You're still going to make Saturday breakfasts for me, right?" He piles toast four pieces high on his plate.

"I hope so. My plan is to drive back from Gloversville on Friday nights so we can be together as much as possible on weekends. Make sure you don't have Ben schedule you to work." I point a spatula in Noah's direction.

"Gotcha. Did Will really offer to stay here during the week?" Six strips of bacon land at the side of his plate.

I nod. "He did. Why?"

Noah shrugs. "I didn't know if you asked Dad to watch out for me, and he said no. I thought maybe you needed another plan."

I put the spatula down on a paper towel. "Absolutely not. As a courtesy I asked your father if it was okay for Will to stay with you. Given Wayne's erratic work schedule, it made sense for Will to be your primary caregiver. Are things okay with you and your dad?"

"Yeah. It's weird. Suddenly he's in my life after not having anything to do with me. He's trying to get to know me. I'm just not sure it's for real." He shoves half a piece of bread into his mouth.

Father, help me. "I'll be honest with you. When I learned I was pregnant, we were kids ourselves. Immature. I didn't handle it well, and neither did your dad. When he rejected me, and then my parents kicked me out, I determined that you and I'd make it on our own. And we have." I walk over to the fridge and bring the orange juice over to the table.

"What changed?"

"Time had a lot to do with it. We matured. When your dad called a few months ago and let me know he was moving to Speculator Falls, he explained it was for more than a job. He realized he failed you. I believe he wants to build a relationship."

"Oh. So you're saying it's always been more about you guys freaking out about being parents than about me being your kid?"

So wise, this child.

I pat his head. "Any rejection between your dad and me or your dad and you has been about the situation, not a person. Certainly not you. And the reason I didn't think to ask your dad to handle things during the week when I'm in Gloversville is because of his work. Besides, Will asked almost as soon as I knew my schedule."

"If Dad calls during the week, can I see him?"

I just want to eat some bacon. I'm not ready for this.

"It would depend on homework and whether you're working at JB's. Your dad knows Will's in charge of those decisions for me. So what he says, goes." I take a piece of bacon and enjoy a quick nibble.

"I know. You remember Dad's picking me up this afternoon, right? You said I could spend the night as long as I'm at church tomorrow." He reaches for another piece of toast.

I nod, drinking in the young man next to me. His brown eyes as big as saucers, like Wayne's. Although my wavy hair disappeared as soon as my pregnancy test was positive, Noah has some curl in his dark hair. Since school started, he's grown four inches. It's hard not to stare.

He catches me looking and starts fixing his hair. "What? Is there something in it?" He touches his chin. "Do I have a zit?"

"No, you're fine. Didn't you say Ben has a new video game available at the store to rent?"

His eyes sparkle. "Yeah. Derek has it, and he said it's amazing. Can we get it?"

There's empty dishes and pans strewn across the table and countertops. Instead of cleaning them, I reach for my purse. "Let's go."

⧗⧗⧗

An hour later, Noah has the car chase game set up, and hands me a controller.

"I don't know how to play. What do I need to do?" I look over the buttons and they're foreign to me.

"It's easy. Use the arrows. Push 'A' to accelerate and 'B' to brake." He presses things that change the television screen until a racetrack shows up.

"Why do I have a funny feeling it's harder than you make it sound?"

Within seconds, a green light appears, a car starts moving, and the sound of screeching tires fills the living room. No matter how fast I hit arrows or push letters, Noah's car leaves me in a trail of dust. His laughter, complete with a cracked voice, rises above the roar of cars.

"Mom, you're in last place. The cop car isn't even bothering to chase you."

We giggle until my car turns around and hits a fence. Then it's full laughter. I glance over and try to remember each sound. The hole in his jeans. The faded Newsboys T-shirt. Even though I'll only be an hour away, not seeing him during the week will hit me hard. Starting school winter semester in the Adirondacks wasn't my smartest choice, leaving commuting out of the question.

Noah looks over. "You okay?"

I rest the controller on my lap. "I'm going to miss you."

He rolls his eyes. "You're going to Gloversville. You're not even leaving the state."

Right. Well, it's going to feel as if we're continents apart.

Before tears can form, three quick knocks come from the front door. I sniffle. "It's Wayne."

Noah drops the controller and springs to the door. "Coming."

The two walk into the living room, Wayne playfully slaps our son on the shoulder. "Ready for our guy's night?"

The two face each other and Noah grins. "Yeah, I am."

I stand and muster a smile. He's wearing a black cable knit sweater and jeans. It's a handsome look I've learned the hard way not to enjoy for more than a second. "Wayne. Hello."

Wayne turns to me. "Hey, Carla. Thanks for letting us do this. Noah and I are going to have a great time." He returns his attention to

Noah. "I wanted to rent this one game that I heard was amazing but——" Wayne notices the television screen. "You have it."

"We rented it. Did you want to borrow it? You couldn't do any worse than I did." I walk over to the console and press eject.

Noah laughs. "Dad, she was the worst."

Wayne chuckles and takes the game from my hand, our fingers touching. "Thankfully she did a much better job in real life driving around for work. She's led more than one ambulance to an accident in snow or fog." He lowers his voice. "The county's going to miss you. Are you really going to become a hairdresser?"

I open my mouth to reply, but there's another knock, followed by a door opening.

"It's me. Will."

"We're in here." I call out.

Will appears a few seconds later at my side. "What are you guys talking about?"

Wayne speaks up. "About Carla's career change. Being a hairdresser."

My boyfriend smiles. "Even I know it's not called that anymore. She's going to be a stylist." He leans down to kiss my cheek. "And she's going to be a great one."

Wayne bites his lip for a moment then turns to Noah. "We should go. Ready, bud?"

Noah holds up his index finger. "Give me a sec to grab my bag." He dashes down the hall.

"Wayne, remember I want Noah at church tomorrow. On time."

"Got it. Anything else?"

Will nods. "Remember, if you have any plans with Noah for the week, call first."

The room feels like the temperature dropped twenty degrees. Wayne turns on his heel and heads for the door without saying a word.

Will playfully nudges my elbow. "So? What do you want to do? We have the evening to ourselves."

I blow out what has to be a batch of hot air. "What was that about?"

He scrunches his eyebrows together. "Huh?"

"Your testosterone-fueled comment toward Wayne. Was that necessary?"

Noah skids to a stop, duffel bag slung over his shoulder. "Everything okay?"

I refuse to look Will's way. "Have a great night, sweetie. I love you."

Noah shrugs and walks away. "Love you, too. See ya, Will."

Once the door slams, Will replies. "He asked if there was anything else."

I roll my eyes and return to my chair. "Wayne was talking to me."

Will lets out a long sigh. "Of course he was. Wayne's always talking to you."

I look up, trying to discern the look on his face. Jealousy? Insecurity?

"Carla, if I was out of line, I apologize. I don't mean to be a jerk."

Neither do I, but fear has a way of bringing out my worst.

My voice isn't much more than a whisper. "Well, you sounded like one."

Will walks over to the couch and plops down hard enough that air squeals out of the cushion. "I'm sorry. It's hard, you know?" He rakes his hand through his chestnut-colored hair. "I don't know where I fit in with Wayne in the picture. He will always be a part of your life because of Noah."

I swallow, but my throat is dry. "Will, this is the first lap of a long race for all of us. Wayne hasn't been a part of my life in fourteen years. Now he is, for Noah's sake. I strongly believe I have to forgive him for the past and trust him with our son. I'm trying."

He clasps his hands together and rests them on his knees as he bows his head. "You're a great mom."

I rise and join him on the couch. "I wish I was a great girlfriend. Sorry I got so defensive." I place my hand on his.

Will lifts his head and slides closer. "You're amazing. You don't give yourself enough credit, either." He chuckles. "I don't give you enough credit. You and Wayne are in the past. Any romance you had is ancient history."

I smile and close my eyes as Will leans in for a quick kiss. But my twitchy fingers still burn from the tingle Wayne gave only minutes before.

⧖ ⧖ ⧖

Two cups of black coffee still don't give me the energy I need to get ready for church in the below-zero temperatures. Usually I'm one of the first in the parking lot, but as I drive down Route 8, a couple thoughts come to mind.

Noah's not with me this morning. My first day of cosmetology school is twenty-four hours away.

As I pull into my usual spot and reach for my purse, I spot Sara Bivins, matriarch of Speculator Falls and Ben Regan's grandmother. Once I leave the car and walk toward her, she waves.

"Carla, dear. Are you ready for the big transition?" She reaches in to deliver one of her famous bear hugs.

Once I get my breath back, we stroll into the church together. "Yes. No. Most of the time. Okay, not really."

She chuckles and reaches for my hand. "It's scary, I'm sure. Career-wise, it's a very different path. You're leaving Noah for the first time. I have a feeling that wasn't an easy decision for you."

Sara's always been such a source of wisdom over the years.

"I know he's in good hands with Will, but you're right. It's hard. I admit, I also feel pressure. What Howard Wheaton did was so generous and gives me the opportunity to have a career with normal hours doing something I love. But I have a fear I'll fail." It's so easy to share with the woman who reminds me of Mrs. Claus with her snow-white hair and rosy cheeks.

"Carla, don't you allow that kind of thinking for a minute. You've been great at everything you've put your mind to. This is the desire of your heart. Don't let any voice but God's lead you."

The sanctuary doors open and Shirley McIlwain is the first to wave us over with the church bulletins in hand. Sara lets go of my hand and marches toward the woman with enormous glasses.

With Sara out of earshot, I whisper to no one particular, "I actually feel guiltier about going away to school because I don't think I deserve it."

⧗⧗⧗

Pastor Craig Reynolds makes a beeline toward me after service. He reaches inside his suit jacket pocket and hands me a business envelope. "Carla, I'm sorry we missed your party. This is a little gift from Brooke and me."

I bite my lip and look to the thick covering. "Do you want me to open it now?"

"Sure." He cranes his neck. "In fact, Brooke has another package for you." Pastor waves her over.

Brooke crushes me in a hug. The envelope gets stuck between us, but her embrace is such an encouragement, I don't mind. "Carla, if you need anything while you're in Gloversville, you just yell. I'll pick up Noah from school, help Will with meals, you name it." She reaches in her purse for an accordion-style folder and hands it to me.

"You both are too much. Will and Noah get along great. They might not do things the way I want them to, but I think Noah will be fine during the week. The biggest hurdle in my mind was Noah's dad agreeing to let Will take care of him. Wayne could have made things difficult." I insert my nail into the envelope and wiggle until it opens. A stack of plastic cards rests inside, and I pull them out.

"That one is from us. We tried to think of something helpful and we thought gas cards were practical. Although you'll stay in Gloversville during the week, it's still a commute back to Speculator Falls." Brooke reaches for her husband's hand.

"This is too much." My voice catches.

"Nonsense. Please take them." Pastor's gaze challenges me as much as his sermons.

"Okay. Thank you." I tuck the cards in my purse.

"Now, this one is from the congregation." Pastor smiles.

I unravel the string and the top from the folder springs loose. A thin sheet of paper is the only contents, and I reach inside.

"This is for rent or anything not beauty school-related. Everyone wanted to contribute."

There are a few zeroes attached to the amount. My hand starts to shake. "Even Kyle Swarthmore?" I need to make light of the situation so I won't cry.

Brooke chuckles. "Yes, he donated. We all wanted you to know we support you. We're family."

Pastor nods. "She's right. We know it hasn't been easy for you raising Noah, and whatever we can do to help, this church is behind you."

The room suddenly feels warm and it's packed with people. "Again, it's so generous. I don't deserve such kindness. I can take care of my son, I mean, it's been just us all these years." My eyes dart around the lobby as I look for a way out.

Brooke releases Pastor's hand and reaches for mine, giving it a squeeze. "Carla, we know you can. You're a great mom. The check is a love note of sorts from your church family."

Church family. Why love someone who became a mom her senior year in high school?

I release Brooke's hand.

Will spots us and saunters over. "I see Carla has the church gift." He places an arm around my shoulder.

"She does, and a little gift from us. Like we told her, if you need any help with Noah, let us know. I'm an empty nester more than willing to lend a hand." Brooke, with her wide smile and ability to get even the most resistant of teens to hug her, is the quintessential mom. Unlike me.

He drops his arm and faces me. "Well, sweetheart, there's another surprise waiting for you in your garage." His eyes are so wide and bright he looks like a kid on Christmas morning.

Wait a minute. I was in law enforcement for years. How did I miss a surprise in the works?

I flash a smile toward our pastor. "I guess it's time for me to head home. Thank you both for everything. I plan to be in church Sunday, so I'll see you then."

Fifteen minutes later, I pull into my driveway. Noah and Will open their doors and sprint toward the garage before I turn off the ignition. *Okay Lord, what are they up to?* My steps crunch as I take tentative steps in the gravel toward the building so small I refer to it as my shed.

"Okay, Mom. Close your eyes." Noah's voice cracks as he calls my name.

"I'm not inside yet." Even after ten years at this property, I can't navigate with closed eyes.

"No worries. I'll guide you." Will sounds closer with each word. Within seconds, he's at my side and taking my elbow. "Noah did most of the work." His husky voice sounds sweet in hushed tones.

"Lead the way."

Once we enter the garage, Noah gives the next instruction. "You can open them now."

I focus on the smiling teenager pointing to a large, wooden, Adirondack business sign resting on a couple chairs.

Carla Rowling: Stylist

"Noah. It's beautiful. You spoil me. Truly, this is gorgeous." I walk over and trace the lettering. A vision of his father giving me a high school woodshop birdhouse flashes through my mind.

Noah clears his throat. "You really like it?"

It's tempting to run over and crush him in a hug. "I love it, and you for working so hard on this." Instead, I walk over and give a gentle embrace, then share the same with Will.

"I can't wait for you to open your own salon." Will spreads his hands in the air. "I can see it now, your storefront. The sign swinging in the breeze."

My breathing quickens. "You forget something. I haven't had one hour of training. I need a thousand. There's a long haul between me starting school Tuesday and unlocking the door to my own shop." Visions of hair color experimenting, perms, and shampoo practice dance around my mind.

"Sweetheart, I believe in you. I'm in for the long haul, too. Nine months is nothing. I'm just putting it out there, but as far as I'm concerned, be ready for me to be by your side for the next nine decades, give or take." Will plants a tender kiss on my forehead.

Those words would be music to any woman's dreams. So why do I feel like I'm listening to rap music at an opera?

Chapter Three

Noah slings his backpack over his shoulder and grabs a banana. "Mom. Seriously. I'm in eighth grade. I've been in the same building since pre-school. You know, down the road? It's no big deal."

I pick up my purse and fish for my keys. "Still, I didn't want to leave for Gloversville until I know you're safe at school."

He sighs. "You're not the sheriff anymore. And this isn't New York City."

"It's not so much about safety. It's that I won't see you until Friday evening." I jostle the keys as I steal a glance at my not-so-little boy. No more Batman backpacks.

"Right. You're living with some old lady during the week."

We walk toward the front door, Noah is only about half an inch shorter than me.

"A widow. Definitely going to be different than what I'm used to."

He nods and jogs ahead, keeping the door open so I can pass by. Once he locks it, he saunters past me. "The late bell rings at eight. I better get moving."

I stop in front of my truck. "Wait. You really aren't letting me drop you off?"

He keeps his pace, but turns back to me. "No, thanks. Have a good week."

"I love you. Don't forget Will's picking you up after school."

I receive a wave in return. What about a hug?

With a sigh, I open the truck door and throw my purse next to one of my packed boxes.

"Love you, too." He calls, his curls bobbing as he walks out of view.

⌛⌛⌛

It's odd driving without a squad car filled with a scanner, siren, and lights. Brad Paisley's newest CD keeps me company as I navigate my 4x4 to the Gloversville address I'll call home for the next nine months.

An hour later, I park in front of an older Colonial with a white picket fence. "Okay, this is it." I reach for my purse and dig out the key the landlord, Betty Cross, gave me when Will, Noah, and I visited the house and signed the short-term lease a few weeks ago.

The woman with silver hair and a kind smile calls from her open front door. "Oh, great. You're here. Come on in, no need for a key." I pause and turn toward her with a smile and wave.

"Betty, hello. I wasn't sure if you'd be home."

She chuckles. "Dear, where else would I be? I'm a bit of a homebody, but so glad you're going to be a boarder here. My sister invited me to play Bunco at the senior center, but I couldn't imagine not being here to greet you."

"That's so sweet. Thank you." With suitcase in hand, I trudge across the snowy sidewalk and up her uneven porch steps.

She keeps the door open, and I notice when I step through that a hinge is loose. Definitely not secure, especially for a widow in town.

Her kitchen table is set with sandwiches and fruit slices. "Are you excited about school? I'm fascinated with your plans. Help yourself, and tell me all about it."

The widow sits and rests her elbows on the table while waiting for me to join her.

I choose a tuna sandwich, take a couple bites, sip some milk, and wipe my mouth with a napkin. "Me? I don't think my schedule is exciting. Maybe different. I'm anxious to get started. Truth be told, I'm restless to get back to Speculator Falls and see how Noah fared without me."

Betty claps her hands together. "That's right, you have a son. Is he staying with your husband while you're here?"

Husband. That term and me never made a lot of sense. The mere mention of the word feels like a stab to the heart.

I cough. "Um, no. I'm not married."

"You poor dear. Do you have a man-friend?" Betty whispers the last word, as if the thought of a boyfriend might be scandalous. She giggles and slaps the corner of the table. "Wait a minute. That young man who accompanied you. Right?"

28

Another dry hack. "Yes. Will Marshall. The one you met." Mr. He-can-see-us-together-for-nine decades.

Betty rises, takes my glass, and refills it. "How nice. But you know, for someone with a great man on your arm and a new chapter in your life starting tomorrow, you seem, oh, I don't know, a little disengaged. Nerves, maybe?" She places the milk in front of me and returns to her seat.

Nerves. Ha. If that's what you call a single mom starting beauty school without any guarantee of succeeding.

"Carla? You okay? If you're tired, you can take a nap, and I'll work on dinner. You need your rest and strength so you can have a great first day tomorrow." She pats me on the arm.

"Tired? Not really, just thinking."

Thinking I'm crazy to believe this dream of mine had any business being my new reality.

⧗⧗⧗

I take a breath before swinging the Gloversville Beauty School glass door wide open. About half a dozen people of various ages mill around the lobby, a wide space full of rich red tones and bright lighting.

"Are you here for the orientation?" A slender, bronze-haired young woman with blond highlights about Noah's height greets me with a clipboard resting on her chin.

"Yes, I'm Sherriff, sorry, wrong career. I'm Carla Rowling." My hair seems dull against the warm interior hues and the perky greeter's own style.

She peruses the clipboard and clicks her pink pen. "Yes, welcome. Orientation starts in ten minutes in the conference room upstairs to the right. Once inside, help yourself to the Keurig machine and bagel and fruit trays. Everyone at Gloversville Beauty School wishes you the best during the next nine months." She flashes a dazzling smile before turning on her six-inch heels to welcome the next person.

The spiral staircase leads to a wing of classrooms. Track lights line the chocolate brown walls. The conference room with a long rectangular white table and ergonomic black chairs isn't hard to find. A small table in the opposite corner holds the refreshments.

I place my purse and notebook on the conference table and walk over to make a cup of coffee. "Sure didn't have a Keurig back at the old office." I mutter.

"I'm partial to the donut-flavored, myself." A man who looks to be about my age holds up his K-cup with a smile, revealing two wide dimples.

I reach for a black mug and look over the variety. "So many choices. I hope choosing my drink is the hardest thing I do all day."

He puts his coffee down and extends his hand.

I take it.

"Hi. I'm Daniel Garrett." He releases his strong grip.

"Carla Rowling. Are you from around here?"

Daniel remains silent as he watches the brown liquid pour into his cup. Once the drink is ready, he turns to me. "Not too far. Lake George. Planning on taking care of the tourists' hair needs. Locals too." His wispy blond locks rest over his eyes. "How about you, Carla?"

"Speculator Falls. I hope to open my own place. We have tourists too, but I think Lake George will have a fiscally higher end clientele." Certain months the tourists in my village wear camo and hunter orange, much like Will.

Daniel nods and waits for me to make my selection and prepare the drink. "That's a lovely area. Are you commuting?"

"I wish, but it's a bit much. I have a room not far from here during the week. It's owned by a widow. I think it will be quiet so I can study. You're probably doing the same, given the distance and winter weather." I grasp my mug full of caffeine and find a seat.

Daniel follows and sits next to me. "Yeah, kind of. My dad lives nearby so I can stay when the weather is bad. Hopefully I can commute later. I have an apartment overlooking the water. Given it's after Labor Day, it will be peaceful around town, too. Good thing, because I want to master these classes. I have a vision for my work." He gestures with his finger. "This school is step one. And I need to be the best here." His smile remains, but his gaze hardens.

Great. One more stressor on my overloaded plate.

☿☿☿

At nine o'clock, the clipboard girl opens the conference room door, ushering in a man and a woman who walk to the forefront of the packed room.

The middle-age woman with exotic features, including high cheekbones, who's wearing a black dress complete with a cape, claps her hands. "Welcome, everyone. Let's not waste a moment of this wonderful journey you're about to begin. I'm Rose Yung, owner and instructor. This is my right hand man and longest serving member of the team, Les Moore."

Thanks to her heels, the man stands a little shorter. With black jeans, a high neck shirt, and a black smock of sorts, he waves.

Chuckles fill the room. I glance at Daniel, who maintains a stoic look.

Les drops his hands to his side. "I know, my parents were hysterical naming me an oxymoron." He laughs. "I'm fun, but what we do here is a form of art. I plan to train you as artists. Your business card means nothing if your clients don't look fantastic. They represent you. They are your publicity. I will work you hard. I will anger and frustrate you. But you will graduate a master."

Rose continues. "As you exit, our executive assistant who greeted you, Brandi, will hand you a personalized folder. It explains your schedule and breaks down your requirements. Part of your class times is instructional, and the rest is lab work." She clears her throat. "Les and I will give a brief summary of the classes and our expectations after Brandi calls attendance." Rose slides a pair of black-rimmed glasses to the edge of her nose.

Brandi saunters from the back to join the speakers, her trusty clipboard with her. "Sandy Brighton." Brandi looks around.

A girl, probably just out of high school, with dyed black hair and heavy eye shadow raises her hand.

"Mitzi Davis."

A bubbly red head springs her hand high in the air. "That's me!"

Brandi nods. "Daniel Garrett."

He responds with a two- fingered salute.

"Carla Rowling."

I clear my throat, but my voice doesn't fully engage. "He--ahem. Here. Sorry."

"Ella Traynor."

No reply.

Brandi scans the audience but doesn't wait before moving on. "Claire Worthington."

The silkiest honey-blonde hair apart from an ear of corn belongs to Claire, who raises her manicured hand.

Brandi smiles and returns the clipboard to her side. "That's everyone. Rose?" The assistant returns to the back.

The owner gazes around the room.

Does everyone investigate faces in their line of work? I thought that was only law enforcement.

"What a bright looking group. We're going to have a great school year, yes?" Rose's smile seems genuine.

Mitzi answers with a resounding yes. The rest of us nod.

Rose releases a soft laugh. "Let's hope everyone finds the passion Miss Davis has. Anyway, your courses are divided by hours. As you know, you need one-thousand hours to graduate. Today, after filling out all the paperwork, we'll offer a tour of the facility. Then, you'll receive a supply list. If you remain all day, you will receive four hours for orientation."

Les continues. "There are thirty hours for bacteriology. If you aren't interested in having an immaculate work station, you might as well leave now."

Thirty hours on health standards and keeping clean?

Rose peers at her notes. "Over 130 hours are devoted to haircutting. Your practicum includes working downstairs with actual clients who want haircuts, perms, color and shampoos. All those are classes as well. Les?"

Les reaches for a tablet. "Let's see. Scalp treatment. Skincare. Manicures. Essential components to a comprehensive salon is the massage area. Facials. But ladies and gentleman, it means nothing if you don't understand the business aspect of running a salon. If you can't recruit clients, charge them fairly and treat them well so they tell their friends and keep returning, then your nine months are going to be a waste of time."

This is more extreme than the brochure I read a dozen times. Almost as intense as the look on Daniel's face. I need to take a jog at lunchtime.

"Questions?" Rose puts her glasses on the table.

Mitzi raises her hand.

Did Daniel just groan?

"Yes. Miss Davis?" Les places his electronic device on the table, too.

"Do all your students graduate? What's your success rate?"

Les and Rose exchange a grin, then Les answers. "Don't be misled. It isn't our success rate as much as it is yours. You get what you give. You give everything you've got, and you will graduate. But...each class tends to have a few who aren't ready for what this school demands. Last year 74% finished, and of those, all graduates passed their state boards for their cosmetology license."

Seventy-four? That's not close to perfect.

I'm far from perfect.

I sigh and look out the window past the parking lot. Will I be one of the students not able to keep up, forced to drop out and disgrace Howard Wheaton's final wishes? *Lord, help me.*

⧗⧗⧗

Five steps inside my part-time home and a plate of cookies comes into view. "How was your first day?" Betty's crystal blue eyes seem to have a sparkle to them.

"Overwhelming. So much information." Visions of scissors, perm rods, and curling irons flash through my mind.

"I thought it might be a long day for you. I made you these. Come. Sit." She leads the way to the Formica table. "So, tell me. How many are in your class?"

I finish the first cookie before answering. "Less than a dozen. One guy seems to be around my age." I reach for another.

"Really? A man in beauty school. Fascinating. What are the teachers like?"

Betty's pretty invested in my day. It feels nice to have her reach out. "Now, Betty, I don't want to talk about me all day. What about you? What did you do while I was gone?"

"Made these cookies and waited for you, dear." She pats my arm.

I wish Jenna was closer. She could give this sweet widow some fun activities to enjoy at the Speculator Falls senior center.

After multiple forced yawns and an empty plate of cookies later, I stretch my arms. "I'm sorry to cut this short, but I have a book list to go over, and I'd like to call home and see how Noah's day was." I stand and push my chair in.

Betty frowns. "Right. Of course. You have a good evening."

As I walk toward my room, I refuse to look back. Don't feel guilty for leaving the room, Rowling. I close the door, pull out my cell, and dial home.

Will answers after the first ring. "So, how was it?"

I giggle. "Hello to you, too."

"Sorry. Hey, honey. How was the first day?"

"So much to absorb and learn. I think I'm more tired from sitting all day than I was chasing down perps running a meth lab." I fluff my pillow armrest and climb on the bed. "You'll think this is funny--I have a teacher named Les Moore."

Will's laughter pierces my ears enough that I hold the phone away until he stops. "That's hysterical. So, how are the other students? Any guys?"

I release a drawn-out sigh. "There's one male student from Lake George. Intense. He has pretty high standards for himself. I don't think any of the others have anything in common except the school. There is a

Goth-looking girl, and a very peppy one. Another has a name so pretentious that I thought I should look for a silver spoon. Claire Worthington." I buzz through each name I could recall.

Will doesn't say anything for a while. "Carla, I think you're applying sheriff techniques. You're trying to get a read on people."

"I mean c'mon, Claire Worthington sounds hoity-toity, and she has luxurious, silky hair that looks like spun gold."

"How would you feel if you learned this Claire was trying to pass judgment solely on your name and hair?"

Gah. Will's moral compass always points to righteousness. "Okay, you're right. Let's say it's a diverse group. The owner seems nice, but I think graduating will be hard. She even said that only seventy-four percent do. That means some from the orientation could walk away." I close my eyes, but an image of me being one of the drop-outs makes me blink.

There's muffled sounds coming from Will's end for a few seconds, and then he speaks. "Sweetheart, you're going to do fine. Howard Wheaton left you full tuition, supplies, housing, and start-up money for a shop because he believed in you. I do too. So does Noah, Jenna, Ben, Sara, Pastor Craig and Brooke...need I go on and list everyone in Speculator Falls?"

I shake my head. "I'm scared."

"You've shut down meth operations. Caught bear trappers. Tangled with domestic abuse cases. You're going to let beauty school knock you to your knees?"

I'm not like the other girls, my track record proved that long ago. "I know you're trying to help. I'm just tired. I have to be up early. Can I talk to Noah, please?"

Another pause, and finally a response. "Sure thing. Carla, I love you."

Oh, how those words flow for Will Marshall. "Right back at ya. Talk to you tomorrow."

Noah's on the phone within seconds. "Hey. I didn't get lost today going to school."

"Funny. I know I treat you like a child sometimes."

"No, I just laugh because our school is so small, just like the area. You worry for nothing."

I shift to the left side of the bed, propping myself on my elbow. "How was your day?"

A long pause.

My policing skills kick in again. "Tell me what happened."

"Okay. A senior stuffed me in my locker. Scotty was there to get me out. Part of the routine. No harm, no foul."

There goes my heart rate.

"You sure you're okay? If you need anything, I can come home. Or, Will or Ben could help you."

"Mom, I can take care of myself. It was a stupid high school prank on the middle school kid. Let's change the subject. How are things for you?"

When did he mature so? "I didn't get thrown in a locker, but I feel overwhelmed..."

"You'll do great." I hear my voice in his words.

"Thanks, bud. Do you have homework?"

"Some. I have a permission slip you're supposed to sign, but since you aren't here, I gave it to Will."

Sharp stabs attack my mama's heart. "You're so grown up. It's like you don't need me."

He lets out a low chuckle. "That will never be true, Mom."

I sit up, feeling validated, loved, and needed. One hour away feels like a million miles apart. "I miss you so much."

"I forgot to tell you last night I'm almost out of underwear."

Out of the mouth of babes. "Will's able to do laundry."

Another pause. "Dad called. Talked to Will."

Hair stands on the back of my neck. "What does he want?"

"He wondered if we could go to Jack Frosty's after school this week. Will's okay with it if I am."

"What did you say?"

"I said it was fine. Dad works crazy hours, so it's cool he wants to grab a milkshake. Say Mom, why didn't you two get married? And, if you don't marry him, are you marrying Will instead?"

Chapter Four

The butterfly feeling that stirs as I pull into the beauty school parking lot reminds me of my high school nerves when I walked the halls wearing maternity clothes. Same dread, wondering if I'll be able to graduate. The worry that people will gossip. This time, I fear I'll mix the wrong chemicals or botch a haircut.

"C'mon, girl. Pull it together. This is first full day jitters. You can do this." I clench the keys in my palm before dropping them in my purse.

"Talking to me, or yourself?" The teen with the Goth look gives a flat smile.

A nervous giggle escapes. "Myself. Not sure why I'm anxious. I was a sheriff before this. I dealt with some pretty tense situations compared to this."

The girl raises her pierced eyebrow. "You were the law?" She walks through the front door with me, and into the reception area. Brandi sits in her chair and smiles as my friend in black scribbles her signature.

"I was." I open my folder and glance at the schedule. Bacteriology. Sounds like a party.

"Did you like it?" She reaches for her folder and looks at the paperwork.

I shrug. "I guess. But it was long hours and a crazy schedule though. Cosmetology was always my dream, and I have a son, so salon hours are definitely appealing."

"That's why you're nervous." She shuts her folder and faces me.

"I don't understand."

"The sheriff thing was a job. Paid the bills. This is a goal, a realization. You want it to work."

"You're pretty smart." We climb the stairs to the conference room.

Her eyes narrow as she spits her words. "For a Goth girl?"

"No. For a girl just out of high school." I smile, opening the door for her.

Three minutes later, Rose Yung in her black stretch pants, blouse, and rose-red scarf glances at her watch, looks at us, and clears her throat. "Good morning. One of the first things you need to know here at Gloversville Beauty School, or as Mr. Moore and I tend to call it, GBS, is that we start on time. You get a two-minute grace once a week. Your clients pay good money to see you. If you can't bother to be there on time, you've spoken..." Rose stops as the class door squeaks open and a woman about my age that I don't remember from the orientation uses her grace day without even knowing.

She takes a seat in the back.

Rose continues. "It speaks volumes about how you value yourself, your job, and your clients."

Our teacher appears to gaze on the latecomer who wasn't at orientation. Rose puts her glasses on, moving them down to the edge of her nose as she places her notes on the podium. "Before we start bacteriology, we need to address the basics of cosmetology."

The model-looking Claire Worthington raises her hand. "Do you mean where the best places to buy supplies are?"

I can't discern if she's being serious or sarcastic, but I hear a few snickers.

Rose chuckles. "Even more basic than that. You need to do these things first in order to move forward. Without them, you'll go under."

Daniel sits two seats down from me, pen in position on top of paper, ready to write.

"You need to be a stylist with outstanding hygiene and grooming." Rose's monotone delivery isn't making for an exciting start.

Mitzi groans. "That's it? Kind of a no-brainer if you ask me."

"You would think, Miss Davis. But I gained new clients because their previous beauticians had bad breath. One male cosmetologist had body odor. Once while I was on vacation, I scheduled a color appointment. The young lady they assigned to me had dirt under her nails. These things are unacceptable." Mrs. Yung scans her audience before continuing. "Let's open your text book to the introduction where we cover these things in detail."

Over the next hour I scribble notes on getting decent sleep and exercise. Eating properly. Staying clean.

Rose walks to the door. "Okay, now on to grooming. Follow me. I have some models downstairs that we're going to examine for their professional appearance."

We shuffle down the staircase and find four people waiting for us in the lobby. Brandi and Les are two of them.

"Okay. You know our executive assistant and lead instructor. The man on the left is my husband, Geoff. On the extreme right is my daughter, Kayla. Daniel, pair up with Carla and tell me the most professional appearance, and be ready to explain why. Sandy, you do the same with Mitzi. Claire, you can partner with our newest student, Ella. Don't be afraid to get close to the models. You have two minutes."

Daniel nods and steps forward, facing me. "So, where do you want to start?"

I look to the left. "How about Mr. Yung? We can go left to right."

We walk in unison to a man with khakis and a white business shirt. The pants have a hole. A small one, but they are the first thing I notice. "I don't think he should wear that for cosmetology. A white business shirt would get hair and color on it after a long day."

My partner gestures a thumbs-up. "There's the hole in the pants. I think that's as unprofessional as the sweat pants you wore to orientation."

Wait. What? They weren't sweat pants.

I clear my throat. "Let's move on to Brandi."

Daniel pivots and leans in to the smiling secretary with her ever-present clipboard. "Her breath is pleasant. No strong odors from perfume or body odor." He steps out of her personal space.

I bite my lip as I study her attire. All black. Nothing missing or broken. Black shoes that looked comfortable. "Well, she looks very well put together. Even her posture is recommended in the textbook."

He keeps moving. "I agree. Let's see the others to make sure." Daniel walks around Les, stopping as they stand face-to-face. "He hasn't shaved. It's not a beard or goatee, just a mess."

Then the hard-to-please gentleman saunters to the last model. Thank God he didn't add personal commentary on the mess part.

I didn't have to move far to share my opinion. "The musk. It's overwhelming." I mouth an apology to Kayla.

Daniel backs up. "Wow. That's pungent. Unlike your fragrance, Carla."

"May I ask what you mean by that?" I join him a few paces away from the models.

Daniel raises his eyebrows. "Um, you smell nice. I didn't think it was that complicated." He releases a slow smile.

"Oh. Thanks." Could this guy be any more confusing? Insult, compliment, repeat.

We share awkward small talk until Rose calls us into a semi-circle near the four models. "So, which model has the most professional appearance?"

Daniel elevates his hand, but speaks before being called on. "Brandi."

The owner doesn't show any feelings of us being correct, or not. "Carla, explain why you and Daniel came to that conclusion."

I look to Daniel, who winks. What is it with this guy? Talk about an enigma. "She's clean, no odors. Her clothes are not only neat, they're appropriate for the work setting. Her shoes match the tone she set with her clothes. Her posture was also closest to what the book recommended. We felt she represented best what we need to emulate." I turn toward Rose.

"Well done. Everyone, Daniel and Carla are exactly right. These are the things you need to choose every day when working with the public."

She dismisses us back upstairs.

Daniel takes the steps two at a time. He stops at the top and turns toward me. "I might be wrong about you."

"Oh? About what?"

"That you weren't cut out for this. I judged you by the drab ponytail you insist on wearing. There might be hope for you after all."

⏳⏳⏳

The next morning Brandi and her funky red glasses are the first to greet me inside the warm beauty school building.

"Good morning, Carla. Ready for shampoos?" She takes a sip from her Gloversville Beauty School mug.

"I guess. Upstairs, right?" I point toward the spiral steps.

She returns her cup to a coaster. "Yes. Mr. Moore plans to have everyone back down here later."

"Oh. We're doing something more than instruction?" I push a stray lock behind my ear.

"Les likes to get right into it. He feels after teaching, it's time to practice. You'll start with the mannequins, then work on each other this afternoon."

I take a deep breath as I head up the stairs. "Great." I can feel sweat beads on my wrist.

Ten minutes later, Les Moore starts class by displaying more brands of shampoo than I can think of on a front table. Daniel, Mitzi, and perfect blonde girl, Claire, rise in their seats, probably to look at the products.

"Ladies and gentleman, if you want a quality reputation, you need a professional shampoo. Most of these here—" The instructor in all black lifts his right arm and with one swoop, knocks the bottles to the floor. "Are junk."

"Whoa. That's a lot of garbage shampoo." Mitzi sits.

"I prefer to call the contents in these bottles perfumed water." He kicks a couple bottles near his feet out of the way. "Now, let's talk about what makes a great shampoo, and then move into the right way to shampoo hair."

Sandy, the girl with dyed black tresses and heavy, dark eye makeup leans in to her left, touching my elbow. "I thought you just stick a head under the sink and lather."

Les looks over at us, so I offer a tight smile. She slithers her elbow back and rests her chin and arms together on her desk.

Daniel, on the other hand, appears to be taking copious notes.

Lord, help me fit into this class and be one of the successful ones.

☖☖☖

When we break for lunch, I stay in my seat and unpack the yogurt, crackers and cheese Betty handed to me in a paper bag before I walked out the door. There's an unlabelled bottle full of some kind of clear liquid. Oh, Betty, so sweet, but I wonder what's in this drink, anyway? Water? Pop?

As I spread everything on my napkin, the woman with a cute blunt cut that I didn't recognize from orientation pulls the seat next to me out, and sits. "You weren't saving a seat for anyone, were you?" She holds up a pink insulated lunch bag.

"No, it's for you. I'm Carla. I don't think we met at orientation?" I open my cracker package and watch her lay out her food with shaky hands.

"I wasn't able to make it. One of those things I couldn't help. I'm Ella Traynor." She unzips a snack bag full of green grapes and pops one in her mouth.

"What do you think of the class so far?" I shift my chair in order to get a better view, and hopefully make eye contact.

"I'm overwhelmed, but trying to calm down. I dread the practice. I'm nervous I'll make a mistake." Ella reaches for another grape.

"I've worried about that too. I'm trying to remember we practice on the heads. Better to learn now than to make an error while with the public. Right?"

Ella straightens and clears her throat, giving me a glance before returning to her meal. "I guess. I hate failing." Her voice catches.

I rotate my chair again, moving closer. Her face is pasty white, quite the contrast against Sandy's painted look and Claire's tan skin.

"Ella, I know we just met, but do you want to talk? I'm a good listener. I can definitely relate to that fear."

She hangs her head until her bangs fall, then jerks up as she pushes the chair back and stands. "No. I'm good. Really. Just stressed. Maybe if Mr. Moore lets us pick partners, we could be a team."

"I'd like that."

The bundle of nerves standing before me reaches for her lunch bag. "I have to make a call. I'll be back. Thanks for letting me sit here, Carla." She turns and walks away.

Strange.

☒☒☒

Once we finish eating, Les leads us down to the salon chairs. He opens a cupboard full of capes and tosses them to every other student. Then he saunters over to where we all cluster.

"Rowling, you and Garrett." Our teacher points to me and Daniel. Great.

Ella grips her cape until her knuckles match her face. I shrug my shoulders, hoping she understands that my gesture means I wish we could be partners.

Les keeps moving. He taps Ella, then uses his other hand to wave Sandy over to join her. That could get interesting.

"Okay, every team take a chair and sink. Cape wearers, you will get shampooed. Your partner will choose the correct shampoo and walk through the steps we went over this morning. You'll be marked for choice and method of shampooing. Once finished, we'll walk through brushes and drying. Then, partners switch and we repeat. Take your places and get started."

We shuffle to a sink. Faucets spew water as I tuck Daniel's cape in to make sure he won't get his clothes wet. He remains silent.

"Oh, one more thing." Mr. Moore raises his index finger.

"Hey! That water is hot." Claire, the flaxen-haired high school graduate jumps up as Mitzi drops the hose.

Les grins. "Ah, I was too late. Get your temperature correct before full immersion. We don't want any burns."

I glance over to Ella, who holds on to the chair as if she's ready to enter a torture chamber. What is her story?

"You're wasting water, Carla." Daniel's voice rises above the water I forgot I was activating.

"Sorry." I test the temperature and start rinsing his hair. "Is that okay?"

"Mmm-hmm."

I take that as approval, so I pour out a dime-sized amount from my selected bottle into my palm. I lather up and pay attention to clean his scalp without scraping him with my nails.

"How is that, Daniel?"

He nods, so I keep the rinse going. When I turn the water off, I open the towel full length and make sure to cover his head and rub. Les is close to my sink, and I feel like he's taking mental notes.

"I'm finished. You can sit up, Daniel, and I guess we wait."

Our professor walks to our area and stands across from me, leaving Daniel in the middle. "Congratulations, Miss Rowling. Your shampoo choice was one of the top three the salon recommends. Your style was effective. Not only a clean shampoo but a focus on your client's comfort."

I exhale.

Daniel pulls on the cape and steps out of the chair to face me. His wet locks don't look much different than the messy style I observed before we started. Wet drops fall on his beard stubble.

"I'm pleasantly surprised, Carla."

I raise my eyebrows. "Sorry? I don't quite understand."

"I'll be honest. When Moore announced we were partners, I wasn't excited. Like I said before, I have a clear vision and it's important for me to excel here."

My back stiffens. "Why would I get in the way of you succeeding? I want to graduate, too."

He chuckles. "I assumed with that sad ponytail you wore last week, and the stringy, limp hair you have today, you don't care about success or your appearance."

My eyes narrow as I cross my arms against my chest. "Do you have a girlfriend?" I ignore the toned muscles in his arms.

Daniel shakes his head. "No, why?"

"I wondered how she put up with you."

Chapter Five

The sixty-plus minute return drive to Speculator Falls helps me shake off shampoo examples, sterilization techniques, and quiz information running through my head and transform me back to being a mom. I put a Taylor Swift CD in the player and try to focus on the weekend ahead, although with the dicey late January weather, I need to watch the road conditions, too.

While navigating the twists and turns that dominate Route 30, my mind leaps forward to the agenda. Helping Noah with homework. Will wants to take me ice fishing. Sunday dinner at Ben's after church, knowing most of that time will be with Jenna talking about the wedding. Happy I didn't have to return to Gloversville until later Sunday.

As I enter the mountain region, suddenly Daniel's remarks come to mind, and my thoughts backpedal from weekend plans to all the sour barbs the uptight guy from Lake George kept throwing my way.

I assumed with that sad ponytail you keep wearing, you have no designs to be an excellent stylist.

That was Monday's kick-off. Several verbal jabs later, he finished the week with *Carla, you need to step it up. Ignoring the same ponytail style you seem married to, you come in looking like you rolled out of bed and stole a mime's clothes. A stylist is constantly marketing their product and advertising their talents. Who will come to your shop when you're in black sweats and wrinkled shirts?*

Looking down at the speedometer, I realize I'm taking out my anger on the accelerator.

Daniel is infuriating. Keeping my mouth shut around him is as hard as remembering chapter two in our bacteriology notes. As I trek north, I have a few comebacks in mind to blast on him when school resumes when my phone rings the *Golden Girls* theme ringtone, my song for Jenna. I click the hands-free device to accept.

"Carla? Are you on your way back?"

It's impossible not to think about her now shoulder-length chocolate color locks. It was a battle to get her to try a new style after years of short hair.

"Yep. I'm almost to Northville. Why? You want a perm this weekend?"

She's fun to mess with.

"You're hysterical. No, I know when we add Ben, Will, and Noah to the mix we won't have a lot of time to ourselves. I wondered how you're doing. It has to be hard being away from your boys all week."

I slow down for a car ahead of me turning left, my mind trying to connect to Jenna's line of thinking. "Boys? Don't you mean Noah?"

There was a pause before she sighs. "Um, Carla?"

"What? I don't understand what you mean."

"Will and Noah. Your boys. Your family, more or less?"

I slap the steering wheel. Will. Of course. "Right. I missed Noah so much it ached, it's been just us for so long I forget to include Will. I can't wait to see them." I was reaching and sense my best friend knows it.

"Is your schooling going any better than your excuses?"

That Jenna never minces words.

⧖⧖⧖

By the time I pull into my driveway, it's dark. The porch light's a beacon leading me to the door. Will's truck is in my usual spot. The scene could be cozy except for Jenna's words running through my mind.

I totally miss seeing Will as part of the family. It's not natural to include him and I can't figure out if that's normal because I've been alone for so long, or if I'm a horrible person for not remembering it's the three of us. Jenna knows my struggle and thankfully doesn't condemn me for whatever I'm feeling or should be. But the guilt plagues me just the same as I walk to my front door.

"Mom! You're back!" Noah throws the door back with such force I'm afraid it will unhinge. He wraps his long arms around me for a rare hug. Even after four days, he seems taller, if that's possible.

"Let her in, Son. She's probably as excited to be here as we are to have her." Will's kind voice filters out the door onto the porch.

Noah jumps up and gestures me inside.

Walking into the living room, everything looks so homey. Even though Betty provides a comfortable room, this is home. I move close to the couch so I can put my purse down and spot a vase full of roses on the coffee table.

Will nearly jogs from the kitchen to greet me. "They're from both of us. We can't wait to hear about your week. Beautiful flowers for our gorgeous lady." Will wastes no time leaning in and planting a kiss right on my lips.

"Will, wow. I guess it was a long week for you, too." I peek at the beautiful bouquet and wrap my arms tight around his neck for another kiss. "Thank you. You take such good care of me." I glance at Noah. "Let me re-phrase that. You take such good care of us."

Will takes a small step back and puts his hands on his hips. "Sweetie, it felt like one of the longest weeks of my life."

Noah looks to the floor, his bangs covering his eyes.

I walk over to my teen. "How was it for you with me gone? Did everything go okay?"

He shoves his hands in his pockets and shuffles with his feet, a habit since his toddler days. One that I remember his father having back in high school. "It didn't smell as nice around here, I guess." He keeps his focus on the floor.

Will joins us. "We did great. But I think I speak for both of us when I say how glad we are to see you home. So, sit down. Tell us everything." He drops on the couch, moves my purse, and gestures for me to join him.

Noah looks to me. "A bunch of kids from school are meeting up at Jack Frosty's for a bit. Can I go?"

I open my mouth to respond, but Will jumps in.

"Your mom just walked in the door. You want to leave now?"

I pivot and face the man wearing faded jeans with holes in the knees. "Will. I can talk to my child."

His smile dissipates faster than fog in the mountains.

Great.

Still, I continue. "Who are the friends?"

Noah's feet keep moving. "You know. Josh. Tommy. Amber. Brittany."

Bingo. Brittany Hunter. On and off crush since kindergarten.

"Jack Frosty's closes at ten. It's after nine. Is that your only plan?"

"We were going to Josh's to play X-Box after." He's moving so much I wait for a tap dance.

That familiar knot in my stomach starts tightening. "Everyone has that plan, or just the boys?"

Noah shrugs. "Don't know. Does it matter?"

I measure my words. "It does. I'm not okay with teen boys and girls alone in a home."

"Josh's dad will be there."

Ugh. I've observed how he pays attention during church.

"You can go to Jack Frosty's. After that, I'd like you to come home." I look up to the boy-man towering over me.

He stops fidgeting. "C'mon, we're just going to play video games." His voice raises an octave despite voice changes.

"I understand, but I was a teen once. Temptation to find trouble is there, and I'm trying to be proactive. If you want to go to Jack Frosty's, we should go." I reach for my purse so I can dig out my keys.

Will stands up.

Noah sighs. "You don't trust me."

Just what I want to return home to.

I fold my arms. "I'm not going to argue with you. Either you're going to the restaurant now, or you're not."

Noah heads to the coat rack and grabs his hoodie. I'm pretty sure I caught an eye roll as he passed by.

Will follows him and he reaches for his coat.

"Will? What are you doing?" My keys jangle.

"Taking him to his friends."

Now my hands are on my hips. "You don't have to. I'm here." Jenna's earlier words feel like the noose against the knots in my stomach.

Will stops so fast he lurches forward. "I want to help."

I suck in a deep breath. The night is spiraling faster than the beauty school staircase. "I know. Thank you. It's just—I miss Noah. I want to spend some time with him."

"Then he should stay here all night and not go out." Will counters.

My hoodie-wearing teen sighs and runs his hand through his hair. "Great."

"Will. I appreciate all you've done, but this is what I do. You don't have to run Noah around now that I'm back."

Will sighs and shakes his head as he zips up his coat. The tan color of his Carhartt jacket offset his eyes, but they aren't filled with the joy I'm so used to seeing. "Carla, you don't get it, do you? And what scares me is I'm not sure you ever will. Or want to."

Noah's eyes widen, and Will pushes on the door, leaving.

Without saying a word.

Chapter Six

With frost etched on my bedroom window, my first thought Saturday morning is, *Forgive me, God. Will being upset with me means I don't have to go ice fishing.*

I procrastinate getting out of bed, the electric blanket is such a comfort in my sixty-five- degree room. I push last night's exchange with Will out of my mind, but then Daniel's taunts take their place. Not the weekend I wanted.

"Mom?" Noah's voice accompanies solid knocking on my door.

"Come in." I click off the blanket in hopes that it motivates me out of bed.

Noah's wearing what he calls his "Saturday sweats," complete with a Giants hoodie. His tousled hair hangs in his eyes, but he brushes it back as he sits at the foot of my bed.

"I'm sorry that our arguing caused a fight between you and Will."

I bite my lip. "Me too, Bud. I'd love to tell you I'm a relationship expert, but I'm far from it. I know worry isn't right, but you're close to the age where I started to struggle and ultimately made selfish choices. I don't want that to happen to you. And with Will, I'm not used to having long term support. I need to work on that."

He pulls the strings on his sweatshirt. "Do you feel bad about your past?"

A sigh escapes as fast as air leaks out of a balloon. "Every day."

"Does that mean you regret me?" He looks to the floor.

A feather could knock me over.

How is it I seem to make things worse so easily?

"Honey. Noah. Look at me." I throw the blanket to the side and slide closer to my teen. Reaching for his chin, I lift it for a moment so we can see eye-to-eye. "I still feel shame that I ignored principles my parents taught me. You know, 'don't awaken love early' kind of a thing. But not you. Not ever. You're the best thing that's happened to me."

A dimpled smile appears. "Josh said there's a girl in Wells that's our age and pregnant. I think of how hard it had to be for you in high school."

Flashes of kids pointing and me hiding during gym class pass my eyes. "You were worth the challenges."

"Are you and Will over?"

I stand and walk over to my robe, fastening it over my flannel pajamas. "No. I don't think so. Maybe. I'm not sure."

Noah nods and heads toward the door. "He's a good guy." His heavy footprints travel down the hardwood hallway. "For someone who always wears hunting gear."

⧖⧖⧖

Leave it to Jenna to orchestrate a gathering later in the afternoon so Will and I can talk.

"I was nervous wondering if you guys wanted to come over to Ben's for dinner. I thought you'd want to be alone, or just the three of you."

I run my fingers through my still unwashed hair. "It was tense last night. Noah even asked if Will and I are through, and I didn't have an answer." I shift the phone to my other ear as I tie my shoe.

"That settles it. Ben will call Will and invite him. You and Noah come over so things with Will can smooth over. Then, we can steal away to Ben's study and work on wedding plans."

A cough rises up from the pit of my stomach. "Wedding? My goal tonight is to get Will to talk to me again."

Jenna's sigh comes through the receiver loud and clear. "Not your wedding, Carla. Mine. Remember? I'm engaged."

Oh. Right.

Three hours after my Saturday run and shower, Noah and I make the trek up Panther Mountain to Ben's massive cabin. We weren't even at the porch to knock when through the bay window I spot Ben wrapping his arms around Jenna and leaning in for a kiss.

"This night isn't going to be uncomfortable at all." I mutter, taking my time to reach the door.

"You say something?" Noah takes the porch steps two at a time and knocks.

"Nothing worth repeating."

Ben opens the door and I'm immediately met with a chili aroma full of onions and tomato sauce. Nothing like comfort food.

"Hey, Carla. Noah. Glad you were able to join us. Will should be here any minute." He takes our coats and hangs them in the closet.

"Great. Thanks."

Jenna rounds the corner and greets me with a hug. "It's so good to see you. I know it hasn't been that long, but I miss seeing you during the week."

"I'm sure wedding planning has kept you busy." I give her a slight push on the arm.

She rolls her eyes. "Guilty. Still, I'm so glad you're here." She takes me by the elbow and leads me to the dining room while Ben and Noah linger in the mud room.

"Hey, Mom. I think I see Will coming up the driveway." Noah's voice deepens, another sign my baby is disappearing.

Jenna lets go and faces me. "Carla, Will is nuts about you. The man is taking care of your son while you're away."

I raise my hands in defense. "I know. I owe him an apology."

A door slams outside just as Jenna squeals. "Maybe we can have a double wedding."

I'm tempted to toss my best friend in the snow to cool her down.

⌛⌛⌛

Making things right with Will doesn't take too long to initiate. He saunters into the dining room, and I realize Jenna's nowhere to be found. Or Ben. Not even Noah is nearby.

"So. About last night." I start as slow as a car on a winter's morning.

Will jams his hands in his pockets. He looks adorable with his trimmed beard. "Yeah. It wasn't quite the homecoming I was hoping for."

"I'm sorry. I overreacted. I'm not used to having someone around to help. I'm also not ready for Noah and his teenage adventures." While I talk, I close the gap between us.

"Carla, I didn't handle last night well either. I'm so excited for you and all God is doing. I know it's a busy time, and I want to help. My hope is that you would factor me into things. Want me to do things just because." He takes his hands out of his pockets and reaches for mine.

"Will you be patient with me as I work on that?" I can barely get the words out with him so close.

"You got it." His voice seems huskier and sends a chill down my spine.

"Forgive me?" I whisper.

"Already have."

Just as our lips touch, the trio that couldn't be found suddenly reappears. I turn to Jenna who gives two thumbs up and mouths, "double wedding."

⧗⧗⧗

Since we spent Saturday evening with Ben and Jenna, Will and I decide to spend time together with Noah after church.

"I make a mean brunch. How about you two come over?" Will zips up his winter coat as others stream out of their pews.

Noah looks to me and nods.

"Sounds good. A full belly might help me forget that I have to leave you two in a few hours."

"We'll be okay. Don't worry." Noah playfully brushes against my arm.

Will chuckles. "I think it's a struggle for her being away all week."

I try to think happy thoughts. A nice landlady, albeit a bored one. School isn't bad.

"It's not like Mom's alone. There's that guy you were talking about." Noah announces, opening the church doors. An icy wind blows through the lobby.

Will closes the doors, keeping us inside. "Huh? What guy?"

The image of Daniel at the sink, flailing his arms around as he brags about being the best shampooer is all I need to share to convince Will there is zero need to worry. Although male stylists have a reputation in their dating preferences, Daniel seems to enjoy the company of women. Except mine. And that's okay with me.

"Daniel's in my class. He's from Lake George. Uptight and arrogant. He can't string two compliments in a row together for me, so really, no worries."

"Do you do a lot together outside of class?" I can't read anything from Will's steady voice.

Noah looks around like he needs an excuse to leave.

I bite my lip as I think. "No, as a group we did a little studying but really, he has the personality of a porcupine." I stand next to Will and give him a peck on the cheek. "There's only one guy for me and it isn't Daniel."

Noah grins. "It's me, right?"

I clear my throat and watch Will study me as he waits for my answer. "Right. Okay, there's only two guys for me."

I promise, I'm going to get this three-of-us thing to sound natural.

Chapter Seven

Daniel looks as serious as a head cold when Les claps his hands first thing Monday and announces the topic of the day.

"Think you know everything about shampoos?"

Mitzi raises her hand. "Yes?" She answers before our teacher can call on her.

"Ms. Davis, it was a rhetorical question. Even so, you're wrong. There is one element to a good shampoo most stylists ignore. It makes the difference between someone who cuts hair to a stylist who gets regular calls. Today is about pressure points."

I try to position myself near Ella but Sandy apparently wants the mannequin with the black hair.

Daniel's smile looks smug as he claims a blond head. "It's true. I heard the best tips go to the shampoo person or stylist that uses pressure points."

I resist rolling my eyes as I find a red head to practice on.

Les takes small steps from left to right, stopping in between to demonstrate. "The stylist uses the perfect balance of gentleness and strength. Now, you try. Remember what you learned last week about shampoos, though."

I grab the sample bottle I feel matches my ginger model. The sink knob sticks, but of course as soon as it gives, water shoots forward.

Daniel's sigh echoes over the water. "You're doing it wrong."

I shut the water off and hiss back. "I know. Pay attention to your station."

"I can't, I'm distracted by being wet. It's more than you turning the water on like a gun shot, you didn't cape your client."

I hate missing the obvious.

Once I rectify that situation, I turn the water on with a bit more finesse, giving my girl a decent soaking. Time to pour a dime's worth of the cleaning product in my palm and begin the process. My hands start near the forehead.

"Miss Rowling, you can sit down." Mr. Moore checks something off on his clipboard.

My jaw lowers, but I obey.

"Mitzi and Claire, you two may also sit down. Everyone else, stop. But remain standing."

My eyes dart back and forth, focused on the standing, and the teacher. I glance at Ella, who keeps her gaze on her mannequin.

"Mitzi, you were doing everything right until pressure points. Don't start at the forehead."

She snaps her fingers.

Les moves to Claire's head.

"You didn't test the water. You easily could have burned your client. You must always test the water. Carla, you didn't cape. Daniel was right."

"Told you." Daniel's sing-song voice isn't appealing.

"The rest of you, you had the correct procedure, including pressure points."

I look at who the winners are.

Ella. Sandy. Daniel.

Les continues. "Let's see. Sandy, you can wash Claire. Ella, take Mitzi. Daniel, that leaves Carla. Those of you getting a wash, pay attention to how the water feels; notice their fingers and the direction they move. Okay, everyone. You may begin."

Daniel remains quiet as he capes me, adjusts the chair, and wets my hair. Within moments I feel strong fingers lathering and circling my skull. I close my eyes. The wider his circular patterns, the more relaxed I feel. I'm nearly asleep when my phone chirps Will's ringtone.

"My phone. It's in my pocket." I wiggle my hand through my right side, splattering suds as I move my head.

"Carla, come on." Daniel's frustrated whine lingers on the outer fringe of my concentration.

I finally pulled the phone out to hear Will's rushed words. "It's Noah."

A minute later, sudsy drops fall to the pavement as I listen to Will while pacing in the parking lot.

"He's okay, but he had a little accident."

My years on patrol processing a scene give my imagination too much fodder. "What kind of accident? Is he okay?" I reach for my hair to run my hands through it, but the wet shampoo stops me.

"He's lab partners with that girl he likes. He wasn't paying attention and mixed two chemicals that he shouldn't have. It produced something of a smoke bomb. They called the paramedics…"

"Wayne." Noah's dad would have the day shift.

Will clears his throat. "Yes. Peterson was on the scene and took charge. Noah's fine. Smoke inhalation and some burning of the eyes."

I walk back toward the building. "Okay, Will. Thanks. I'll be there as soon as I can."

"Carla, wait. Wayne asked me to call you just so you'd know. He assured me all was well and you weren't needed. I, uh, believe him. The part about Noah being okay."

I close my eyes and make a fist with my free hand. "He was in a chemical related accident. It sounds like they have him here in Gloversville. I can get in my squad…" A stray tear falls down my right cheek as reality hits. "Right. I'm not a sheriff. But as a mom I can be there…"

"Sweetie, Noah truly sounded fine. If anything, he's getting attention from Brittany because he got hurt on their project. She was at another table comparing notes with her best friend. Do you want me to do anything?"

I sigh, brushing away the tear. "I'll call Wayne and let you know. If Noah wants to stay with his dad, I'm okay with it." But I am going to see my boy.

"Works for me if it works for you." Will, always so good-natured.

"It does. For now. Thanks for calling."

"Anytime. Don't worry. I know it's hard. And Carla?"

I flex my hand. "Yes?"

"I love you."

I hang up before I can reply, my feet already back inside the demo area.

All eyes seem to zoom on me, even as I return to my station in hopes Daniel can rinse my hair.

Les speaks before Daniel. "Everything okay, Miss Rowling?"

"No. I mean yes. My son had an accident at school."

Mitzi's eyes widen. "Oh my goodness, is he okay?"

"I've been told he is." I look straight at my teacher.

"Do you need to be excused to find out for sure?" Mr. Moore's eyes seem compassionate, like a father. Unlike my dad.

"Thank you. I'll feel better seeing for myself." I turn around and face Daniel. "You can finish."

Daniel nods and turns the water back on while I lean back into the sink. After a few seconds he returns to massaging my head, rinsing the suds out. As relaxing as his magic fingers are, I can't stop thinking about Noah. Wayne. Will.

"I hope everything is okay with your son. Is he here in Gloversville?" Daniel's voice is barely audible above the water.

I rise, but his grip on my head strengthens. "Yes. Smoke inhalation and burning in his eyes."

The sink shuts off and a thick towel suddenly sits on top of my head. "My father is an ER doc there. I can call him, if you'd like." Daniel's voice sounds soft and kind.

I balance the towel as I sit up. "You would do that?"

He shrugs. "It's an emergency, right?"

I nod, my towel bobbing. "The crisis is over, but I guess it's a peace of mind thing."

"While you were outside Les said we were dismissed once the wash is over. Tomorrow you wash me, based on what you learned from my doing your hair. I can call my dad now."

I bite my lip, willing the tears not to flow. "Daniel, thanks. I really appreciate it."

He gives a reassuring smile and starts dialing.

⧖⧖⧖

Forty-five minutes later I thank Dr. Garrett for explaining Noah's eye care and then I text Daniel to thank him for putting me in touch with his dad. I'm about to open the curtain to Noah's area when my phone beeps.

No problem. See you in the morning. -D

With phone put away, I peek through the curtain. "Hello---someone wanting their mom?"

Noah coughs. "Dad, did you call her? I told you I was okay."

Once I step inside I notice Wayne in the corner, holding what looks like eye drops.

"Hey. Carla. I knew you wouldn't be able to stay away." My former boyfriend grins and looks to our son. "Will called her."

"You're crazy if you thought I wasn't going to check on you. Are you sure you're okay? That's quite the cough." I lean in and kiss Noah's forehead, careful not to touch the eye covered with gauze.

Noah sits up and sighs. "I'm fine. Dad's going to look after me. Just eye drops and lots of water for my throat."

I look to Wayne, who nods.

"He really is fine." He reaches out and rubs my arm, which sends a shiver through me.

I return my focus back to Noah. "Are they able to release you soon?"

Noah nods. "Just waiting on discharge papers. I get to stay home tomorrow from school. Brittany promised she'd bring me my homework and read stuff to me if my eyes hurt."

Wayne chuckles. "If it's okay with you, he can stay with me. I need to give him drops every so often. It makes sense. I promise I'll take him back to your house..."

"I know. It's okay. I feel bad I can't be there. Maybe I can drive back and forth."

"Mom. That's crazy. It's winter. We get like a foot of snow every day. I'm good."

I sigh, knowing he's right. But I still feel guilty. "Okay. I'll stay until you're discharged. You can tell us all about Brittany." I wink.

⧖⧖⧖

It's dusk before the three of us exit the ER. Noah's still chatting about Brittany as Wayne balances the eye drops and salve and I handle the triplicate paperwork.

"Where are you parked?" Wayne asks.

"Probably near you. I'm so used to being in a sheriff's car that I almost parked in the emergency vehicle area."

He nods, heading toward the middle of the small, square lot. "That would be a hard habit to break. Quite the switch from law enforcement to hair."

We stroll toward the third row. "A blessing, really. From doing what I had to and now, what I want to." I see my car. "Oh, I'm over there."

We stop and I wrap Noah in a hug. "Please do what your father says."

"I will."

I wave and start for my car.

Wayne's voice trails behind me. "This was nice, right? The three of us. Kind of like we're a family."

As soon as I see him drive away, I slump into my seat and cry

Chapter Eight

Betty wraps her shawl tight around her neck. "There you are, Carla. I was getting worried. I thought maybe I'd see you last night. Or this morning. Then I thought perhaps this afternoon." Oh, Betty. I totally forgot to check in. Another person I'm not including. Sigh.

I force a smile and gesture for her to go inside. "I'm sorry. It's been crazy." I follow her. "It was a late night, so I used my entrance. It was important to get to school early; things are out of sorts. My son had an accident at school."

Betty gasps and covers her mouth. "Oh, dear. What happened? Is he okay?"

"Yes, he's fine. It was a lab mishap. His father is a paramedic, so I thank God for the quick care he received. They transported him to the hospital here to make sure he was okay. I got to see him, but it made for a long day." I start toward the hallway when I hear her soprano voice.

"But I made a pumpkin roll."

Pressure points radiate from my head; the same places I need to memorize for morning class. Betty's like the mafia. There's no saying no to her.

"One small piece. If I keep eating dessert I'm going to gain 50 pounds."

Betty claps her hands together and scurries to the kitchen.

⧗⧗⧗

Half an hour later, I'm done eating and am now wearing sweats with my hair in a ponytail, ready to tackle my textbook. I stifle a yawn, knowing as soon as I refresh my knowledge on pressure points, it's time to start the anatomy and physiology of skin, hair, and nails. Joy.

I conquer reading as far as skin and infection when next thing I know, I nod off. My Galaxy phone startles me back to reality. I reach for it, near my neglected textbook.

"Hello? Carla?"

I try to guess the voice, but my brain seems to be half-asleep. "Yes? Who is this?"

The low chuckle makes me sit straight up.

"Wayne? Is that you? What's wrong? Is Noah okay?"

Another laugh. "Relax. Everything's fine. He's using the eye drops and is currently fast asleep in the spare room."

My shoulders relax. "Okay, good. So, you called to let me know?"

"That's part of it. You've been good at keeping me informed since I, uh, moved back and into your lives. I also had a question."

"All right. What's going on?"

"I'll be in Gloversville Wednesday. Wondered if we could meet. I think it needs to be in person."

My stomach tightens as I imagine the possible reasons why Wayne would want to meet. He wants custody of Noah. He's moving away again. He's dating someone and wants Noah to meet her.

"Carla? You still there?"

"Yes. Sorry. What time are you thinking? I'm in class until four."

"How about four-thirty at Harold's? My treat, and I figured you'd want Noah back with Will by then, so I don't have to race home."

I can't tell if there's a hidden meaning in his comment. "That works. I guess I'll see you then."

Once we disconnect, my mind races into overtime. By the time I finish my reading, the only scenario that makes sense is Wayne wants custody. The mere thought keeps me up past three in the morning.

My blue tights on, and I'm off for a jog by seven.

⏳⏳⏳

Leave it to Daniel to speak up as soon as he sees the bags under my eyes at our first class Tuesday morning.

"I hope that tired look is because Les asked you to be a live skin demo, and not because you had a rough night with your son." He attempts a smile, but not a very convincing one.

Mitzi waltzes into the classroom and right up to me. "Wow. I could shop with the bags under your eyes."

"Okay, hint taken. I didn't get a lot of sleep." I turn toward Daniel. "But my son is fine, thank you."

Before the peanut gallery surrounding me can say anything more, Les strides in and places a stack of papers on his lectern.

"Okay, class. Quiz time. Let's see how much you know about pressure points before we move on to anatomy and physiology."

My head pounds like a carpenter's hammer, I'm pretty sure I could be the live demo for all Les is going to teach today.

⏳⏳⏳

Daniel's the last to hand in his quiz. Les looks at the clock as he holds the papers.

"Why don't we break early for lunch? I'll grade these, and Rose will be ready to start the new unit this afternoon."

Claire stands and turns toward me. "Want to go somewhere, Carla?" She looks to the long table where Mitzi, Sandy and Ella sit. "Ladies? Care to join?"

I shrug. "I'm game."

Sandy adjusts her leather jacket. "Hot dog place?"

"Sure." Claire clears her throat. "An offer that good means I'll buy, if that helps." She smiles.

Ella glances my way before replying. "I guess I could. As long as we're back in time."

We stand and gather our coats and purses while Daniel sighs.

"No, no. Don't ask me. Just because I'm a guy."

Claire puts her hands on her hips. "I thought about asking you, but then I wondered how we could talk about you with you there?"

I'm not sure whose smile shocks me more—Ella's or Sandy's.

Daniel doesn't miss a beat as he picks up his coat. "Please. You're going to talk about me whether I go or not. You've got the money, I might as well tag along."

⏳⏳⏳

Thirty minutes later, our little class is at the hot dog joint, enjoying our meals. Mitzi's the one asking questions between bites.

"Okay, Claire. I need to know. Why beauty school? Why here? Something tells me if you asked your family to send you to Paris, they'd do it."

Sandy coughs. "Wow. Way to be subtle."

The corn-silk-haired beauty rolls her eyes. "Just because my clothes don't come from the discount store doesn't mean I'm a spoiled brat. If we're going to judge on appearance, why is Sandy here? She looks ready to go to some grunge band reunion."

"Hey! I didn't start this conversation." Sandy puts down her fork. "Besides, you didn't answer the question."

Claire picks up her napkin and dabs the edges of her mouth. "Okay. My mom was a stylist before she met my father. She went to school here."

Daniel nods. "Boy, I know that story. Your parents want you to follow in their footsteps."

Did Dr. Garrett want Daniel to go into medicine?

Claire pushes her salad plate away. "No, that isn't it. My mom died last year. I want to honor her memory by doing what she loved. I'm nervous I won't be as great at hair as she was. If you guys can help me, I'd appreciate it."

Mitzi gasps and blinks back tears. "I'm so sorry. I never would have asked if I'd known."

Ella shifts in her chair. "I wish I had confidence in my abilities. I'd help you."

"Maybe if you relaxed? You seem kind of tense all the time." Sandy shoves the rest of her chicken tender in her mouth.

I glance at Ella, who tucks a piece of hair behind her ear. "I do? Sorry. I'll work on it. This is new. I've been home with the kids since their births. I need…"

Ella's phone rings and she nearly dives inside her purse to retrieve it. She glances at the front and immediately stands. "I'm sorry. I need to take this."

Despite the winter temperature, the nervous mom dashes outside.

"What's that all about?" Claire cranes her neck toward Ella.

"Maybe one of her kids needs something." Mitzi offers.

I dip my last French fry in ketchup and say nothing. Because my sheriff's imagination is reeling from the almost-hidden sight of Ella's fading black eye.

⧗⧗⧗

By Wednesday afternoon I'm dragging out of our anatomy and physiology class and dreading meeting Wayne. The week's been full of worrying about what he wants, wondering what is going on in Ella Traynor's home life, and fighting boredom in this class.

"You're still wearing those grocery bags under your eyes." Daniel gives a playful shove with his elbow as we walk downstairs toward the lobby.

"You sure know how to make a woman swoon."

"I'm just concerned. I want to make sure nothing's wrong. We tied for highest score on that quiz, by the way." He fiddles with his keys as we exit the building.

"Right. You'd love for something to be off so you could zoom to the top of the class."

I reach my car first and start to unlock it as he keeps walking, but he gives a wave.

"Okay, enjoy those dark bags Carla."

⧗⧗⧗

Wayne motions to me as soon as I walk into Harold's, ten minutes after leaving the school. My stomach clenches as I move closer to the table.

"Thanks for meeting me." His voice is steady and non-threatening, but my heartbeat still accelerates as he stands and pulls out my chair for me.

"I confess, I'm curious why you wanted to meet."

He chuckles as he sits. "I didn't mean to sound mysterious. I know you're in town for school during the week. I had to be here for work. I've had something on my mind, and after the other day with Noah, I thought I should say something."

Wayne hands me a menu and starts looking at his.

I place mine on my plate. "Is it about Noah?"

He lowers the menu. "Not really. You're nervous about this?"

"I am. Please. I can't even think about eating until you tell me."

A waitress walks up to our table and pours water into our glasses.

"We need a few minutes before ordering," Wayne instructs.

She looks at me and nods before walking away.

Wayne folds his hands together and puts them on the table. "Okay, we can talk now. It's going to sound crazy, but after the three of us being together at the hospital, I felt like I had to say something."

I try to swallow, but my throat is so dry I can't. "Say what?"

"I was a jerk for walking away when you needed me most. And you were amazing to allow me back in Noah's life when I moved here. I thought you'd take me to court or ban me from seeing him. And I deserved that. But, you've been great." He takes a sip of water. "I love being with him. There was something I said the other night that I can't get out of my mind."

My mind races trying to recall everything he said, but I'm at a frantic loss.

"Carla, I lost out on a wonderful thing when I walked away." He shakes his head. "Fourteen years without you both, but we looked like a great family at the hospital, didn't we?"

"I don't understand." My teeth nearly chatter from nerves.

He sighs and reaches for my hands. "I know you're with Will Marshall. But he doesn't have what we have. We have a child. The guy doesn't seem to have permanent intentions. Or, if he does, I don't see where it's mutual. So, until I see that change, I want to throw my hat in the ring."

"What?"

"I'd like you to consider me. You and me. We had something great as kids, and I'd like us to try again now that we're adults. Doing things the right way, of course. Carla, I think we have something, and I'd like to explore it."

Chapter Nine

Even with a late January snowfall, the Friday evening drive back to Speculator Falls is a welcome relief. Wayne's confession still stuns me, even after two days. I need time and space. Leave it to Jenna to call in hopes of finding out the latest.

"Any chance we can catch some girl time while you're home?"

I navigate past a snow drift. "Is it to talk about Wayne?"

"No, but since you brought up his name, there must be something to talk about. What's going on?"

Concentrating on the snow-covered roads helps me be matter-of-fact. "Wayne wants me to dump Will so we can be together."

A high screech flows through my speaker. "No. Way. Carla, it's like a soap opera with you. What did you say?"

"I was in complete shock. I fumbled around, asked for the check, grabbed my sneakers, and ran three miles."

My best friend chuckles. "For a former sheriff, you sure take off a lot when the going gets tough."

I'm now in the hamlet of Hope. Which I could use massive doses of.

"Okay, touchy subject, I get it. How about something else? Say, my wedding? Think we can steal some time away so we can plan? Ben's antsy. He's more than ready, and I keep putting him off because I don't know how to execute a wedding between my Ohio life and my Adirondack one."

I flashback to my first meeting with Jenna. City girl with lowlights and an even lower car that didn't survive the mud and her steep driveway. It didn't take her long to acclimate to Adirondack life. I understand her wedding planning conflict.

"I didn't even think of that. You're such a natural around here I forgot you're from Youngstown. That is a problem."

"Can you help me think it through? It would mean a lot." Her voice softens, and it's impossible to say no. The romance between her and Ben is the happiest story to come to Speculator Falls in a long time. Even

Will admits the evolution from rivals to best friends who are now engaged beats our quiet courtship.

"How about I come over tomorrow morning? Noah has basketball, so I'm free."

There's a giggle on the other end. "Sorry, Carla, I can't help it. I'm glad you can help. But with two men vying for you, you sound anything but free."

⧖⧖⧖

Noah and his eye patch are the first to greet me when I pull into the driveway. He opens the passenger door and lifts my suitcase.

"Hey, Mom. Welcome back. Did you have a good week, aside from visiting me in the hospital?"

Visions of his father confessing his romantic feelings for me come to mind.

"It wasn't bad. Long, but it always is when I'm apart from you."

We walk side-by-side to the front door, passing Will's truck.

Noah sighs. "Say, there's this dance at school next week. Kind of a winter thing, I guess. Brittany said she was going, so I wondered if I could go."

I reach for the handle but turn toward him. "Did she ask you to go with her?"

Please say no.

He kicks at some snow. "Not in those exact words, but Chad thinks maybe she'll dance with me. It's next Friday, so you'll be in town if you're worried."

His baby face is disappearing. I almost think I see chin stubble. With the door open, I gesture for him to get out of the cold.

"I guess so. I'd rather one of us drive you, though."

In the kitchen, Will puts down the skillet and heads toward us. "You're back. I didn't hear you pull in." He opens his arms and gives me a bear hug. "Where are we driving?"

Noah clears his throat. "School dance. Mom said I can go. Brittany's going to be there. I really want to go. Dad told me dances were the best times for him. Especially with you, Mom."

I offer a small smile and look at the floor, wishing it would open and swallow me up.

⧖⧖⧖

After dinner, Noah heads to his room and that gives Will and me time alone on the couch. He wraps his arm around my shoulder and gives a squeeze.

"Before I head home, how was your week? Anything interesting happen? I'm sorry I was called away to Utica for a couple deliveries. I missed checking in with you."

My hands turn clammy as I face him. "Funny you ask, because…"

He leans forward, a mischievous grin spreading. "Did I ever tell you how much I love your smile?"

I'm just as mesmerized as I stare into his mint green eyes.

He starts the kiss, and for a couple seconds I forget I have to tell him about my week.

"Will, wait." I move back.

He chuckles and grasps my shaking hand. "I know."

"You do? How?"

"I guess when you feel the exact same way, you understand it when you see it."

Wow. I don't give him enough credit for being understanding.

"So, you want me to explore this?" I wipe my hand on my sweater.

His eyes widen and he pulls me in for a tight hug. "Honey, I can't think of anything I'd like more."

Wait. What?

"Will, I'm not sure we're talking about the same thing. What do you think I mean?"

"That cliché is true. With you gone during the week I realize how much you mean to me. Absence does make the heart grow fonder. Looking at the expression on your face, I believe you're ready to say you love me as much as I love you. And that it won't be long before there's another engaged couple in Speculator Falls."

A nervous laugh evolves into a hacking cough. I jump from the couch to get a glass of water and spot my sneakers. If I skid to a stop to put them on and run, would it kill the mood? If so, is that so bad? Because the expression on Will's face resembles a lovesick puppy. And I just plain feel sick.

"Carla? You okay?"

I paste a smile and try to find a giggle among the hacking. "Yes, swallowed wrong." I ignore the running shoes and get the water. After a couple swallows and a few deep breaths, I return to the couch.

"Did my confession make you cough?" Will grins, leaning in for a kiss.

"It was a little unexpected." I hope returning the affection distracts him. I'm not ready to explore my feelings. Especially when I need to confess Wayne's proclamation.

"I don't mean book the church for next week. I know you've had a lot of hurt through the years and you've said we need to go extra slow. We're in a good place even with the distance. Wouldn't surprise me if we, you know, make this last."

His explanation calms my heartrate, and I reach for his hand and lace my fingers through his. "Thanks, Will."

"For what?"

"Being you. Understanding me. Believing in us."

He chuckles and squeezes my hand. "You make it easy."

And to keep things simple, I settle in on the couch, holding his hand, and deciding this isn't the time to tell him about Wayne's feelings for me.

⧗⧗⧗

After stopping at The Four Corners for donuts Saturday morning, I knock on Jenna's door. She opens it and I'm impressed to see her brunette hair in a high ponytail.

"I'm so glad you're here. I know you're going to be so much help with the wedding." Jenna gives me a quick hug.

I lift the donut bag. "I thought a sugar rush would help."

Jenna grabs the sack. "You're so smart." She ushers me inside. "Mocha? I cleaned my machine and the frother is ready."

That girl and her fancy coffee.

"No, thanks. Once you've worked in the sheriff's office, it's hard to drink anything that uses a frother." I take off my coat and place it on the back of one of the breakfast nook chairs.

She sits on the couch. In front of her, the coffee table's stacked high with wedding magazines. A trace of glaze sticks to the edge of her mouth. "I don't know why I can plan all the events at the senior center and can't decide on anything when it comes to my own wedding. Mom offered grandma's dress, so I at least have that. But nothing else."

I sit beside her and grab a chocolate iced cake treat. "So, you don't know the date? The colors? The bridesmaids?"

Jenna brushes sugar off her jeans. "Carla, I don't even know where to have the wedding. My family is in Ohio. My friends and my life are here."

"Okay. I have an idea. Close your eyes." Jenna closes them, then they pop back open.

"Are you going to eat the rest of the donuts?"

I roll my eyes. "No, silly. Just do it."

She sighs. "Okay. Done."

"Take a couple seconds to focus."

Jenna takes a deep breath and exhales.

"Now, I'm going to say a quick prayer." I shift so I'm even closer to her. "Heavenly Father, we ask that this be a productive meeting this morning. Help Ben and Jenna have the wedding You desire them to have. More than that, be the head of their marriage. Guide them in all things. Give Jenna clear direction on the plans she needs to make today. Thank You for all You have done, are doing, and are about to do in her life. Amen."

She opens her eyes. "Thanks. I've been running around so much; I didn't even have the sense to pray about the wedding plans."

"Were you able to picture the wedding? Is there a particular season you imagine it taking place? Can you see yourself at a church, or outside? Anywhere specific at all?"

Jenna nods. "It's funny you ask. When you said the prayer, I could see Ben and me at the altar. Here, in Speculator Falls. I've wanted my parents and Meg to see where I work, and where Ben and I will live. I guess there's no better time for them to visit than for my wedding."

I smile. It feels good to see plans come together for my best friend. As she continues to talk about them, I think about my own situation with Will and Wayne both declaring feelings for me. I wish I could have answers as fast as Jenna.

"I hear a car coming up the drive. Probably Sara. She said she might stop by." Jenna stands and walks over to the door. "It's her. I'll be right back. I'll see if she needs help."

As long as I've known Sara Bivins, she's rarely needed help. She's the matriarch of Speculator Falls and is always helping others. Jenna's going to have an amazing grandmother-in-law.

The two enter the house and Sara waves. "Hello, Carla. How's beauty school?"

I stand and offer her my seat. "Busy, but good. This week we start haircutting."

Sara sits and pats her snow-white hair. "Great. I'm due for a trim. You can always practice on me."

Jenna carries a chair from the breakfast nook and places it across from the couch, so I can sit. "Carla helped me realize I want the wedding here in Speculator Falls. And you know, it was April when I moved here. Met Ben. I'd like to get married then." The ideas keep coming.

Sara claps her hands together. "April. I love it. A new beginning, especially here in the Adirondacks as the snow starts to melt away and new life begins to shows up. If you want, I have a friend in Glens Falls that does beautiful arrangements with the mountain bluet. It's the perfect Adirondack flower for spring. I'd be happy to pay for your flowers as my gift to you and Ben."

Jenna leans over to give Sara a hug. "You're such a blessing, Sara. I'd like to make that the color of the bridesmaid dresses, too. You two are the best. Everything feels like it's coming together, and I owe it to both of you."

With a meager smile I sit back and listen to Jenna and Sara plan. I close my eyes for a moment, trying to picture my future, and the man in it. Thing is, thanks to the overwhelming reality that two men have declared feelings for me this week, the only image I can conjure is me and Noah.

⧗⧗⧗

Weekends fly by even faster now that I'm in school and living elsewhere during the week. Already church is over and although I need to go home and pack, I linger at the altar. I never thought I could relate to Queen Esther, but Pastor Reynolds gives ample proof the orphan struggled with making the right choice.

"Hi, Carla. Is there anything I can pray with you about?" Brooke Reynolds rests her hand on my arm.

"My decisions aren't quite life and death, but I have choices to make that affect a lot of people. Most of all, Noah. I don't want to mess that up." My voice catches on the emotion building within me.

"You know what impresses me in Esther's story? It's so simple I missed it for a long time." Brooke's smile is so warm and comforting, I'd love to talk with her all day.

"I don't know. Her courage?"

"She certainly possessed that when the time to act was on her. No, I'm thinking more about the King. He had four hundred women to choose from. Those women had a year to prepare through beauty treatments and training. He chose Esther because she wasn't like the others. She was set apart on so many levels, and Xerxes saw that in her."

Out of the corner of my eye I see Will wearing his favorite bright orange hunting jacket.

"She could have played it safe, but she didn't."

Question is, what's safe? The father of my son that I don't think I love? Or Will, the teddy bear who would move mountains if I asked him to?

"That's true, Carla. What motivated her to do the right thing was she took the time to pray, and she asked everyone else to do the same. It made all the difference."

Prayer. My challenge to Jenna.

"Do you mind if I take a moment to pray for you?"

I nod and close my eyes.

Brooke moves her hand to my shoulder. "Father God, Carla needs to hear from You, and how You long to lavish your love on Your daughters. Give her wisdom from heaven. Peace that passes all understanding. And a covering through the process that would protect her and Noah from the true defeated one. We give You the glory, Lord. It's in Your name we pray, Amen."

"Thanks, Brooke. I'm going to keep praying and trust God to show me."

Will walks toward me, and my stomach does a mini flip as he stands next to me.

"He's faithful, Carla. He'll give you exactly what You need."

I know Brooke means God, but I feel like it could be the same answer when I think about Will.

She smiles. "You two go on, I know you need to get back to Gloversville." Brooke winks and walks away.

Will squeezes my hand. "You okay?"

I look up into his soft green eyes. "I'm getting there."

We walk to the lobby in search of Noah, still hand-in-hand.

"He might be in the youth room. I'll check."

As I approach the area where I think Noah's at, a man turns the corner and smacks into me.

"Carla. Sorry, I didn't see you." He reaches for my arm and doesn't let go.

"Wayne? What are you doing here?"

Chapter Ten

Wayne's tousled hair and dazzling smile take me aback as much as his presence at church. "I didn't have to work today, and Noah's been asking me for months to attend. I was actually looking for him."

I lick my lips in an effort to find words and say them. "Me, too. I think he helped in the nursery during service. That's great that you used a free morning to be here."

Wayne squeezes my shoulder. "Carla, I mean everything I've said. I'm committed to creating a lasting bond with my son. And, if you'll have me, I'll make sure I treat you as the amazing woman you are. I should've acted that way toward you from the beginning."

My shoulder radiates heat even after Wayne removes his hand. Before I can reply, Noah walks up behind him.

"Hey, Mom." He looks to the man wearing a paramedic coat. "Dad! You came!"

Wayne turns and hugs Noah. Just as I pivot and face the lobby, Will walks up.

"I wondered where you were. Wayne? I didn't know you were here." Will smiles and offers his hand. The two men shake. Noah stands still, his eyes darting back and forth between us.

"Will, good to see you. I had today off and thought I'd take Noah up on his invitation. So, you and Carla are spending the day together?"

I cough as soon as I hear my name.

Will doesn't seem to notice my growing anxiety. "We are. And you know, Wayne, you've been so kind in letting me watch Noah when Carla's away that I want you to be one of the first to know."

I clear my throat. "Know what?" My voice sounds more like a screech.

Will drapes his arm around my shoulder. "Carla and I are giving serious thought about our futures. I think you can expect a wedding announcement soon."

No. I'm not ready for this. I could entertain the thought on the couch. But this?

Wayne's smile disappears. "Really? The talks have been recent?"

My heart feels like a basketball pounding double-time down the court.

Wayne clears his throat. "She's a great catch, Will."

Will's beaming. "That she is. I promise I won't disrupt the good thing you have with Noah." He steps away from me and shakes Wayne's hand again, then reaches for Noah. "Hey, bud. Let's give your parents a minute. We can head to the car."

Noah looks back and forth between me and the two men. Is he as conflicted? Or, is he relieved to finally have some men in his life?

The two walk away.

"Are you sure, Carla?" Wayne barely whispers.

I take a breath and try to speak, but nothing comes.

So, I turn and sprint away the best I can in my dress shoes.

⌛⌛⌛

I'm still anxious thinking about Will's declaration and how gracious Wayne seems. My entire drive back to Gloversville, confusion jumbles my thoughts. Did I make the right choice? Then it hits me, I didn't really say anything. Groaning, my breakfast lurches in my stomach. Did I really stand there and do nothing? Yep. That was me.

When I enter the lobby area first thing Monday morning, Brandi hands me a coffee mug with the school logo on it, full of brown steaming liquid.

"Good morning, Carla. Ready to start haircutting? Rose wanted everyone to know these mugs are for you to keep. A little something to encourage you." Brandi pushes her glasses up the bridge of her nose.

The cup is warm against my hands and the contents a balm against my dry throat. "I'll have to thank her. My guess is you made the coffee, so I appreciate that, too. Although, I probably shouldn't drink too much or I'll get jittery."

Brandi giggles. "No worries. You're just using the heads today."

I smile and walk upstairs to the classroom.

Mitzi, Sandy, Daniel, and Claire are already in the room and seated.

"Hey, Carla. Did you have a good weekend?" Mitzi waves me over.

Define "good."

"It was interesting. What about you guys?" I place my drink on the table between Daniel and Claire.

"Boring. I worked all weekend at The Taco Shack." Sandy rolls her eyes.

"I babysat." Mitzi reaches for her textbook inside her backpack.

"I read the textbook." Daniel offers.

All heads turn in his direction.

"You went through the entire thing?" Claire's eyes widen.

Daniel shrugs. "You ladies don't understand. I have to be an amazing stylist. Do you know how many strikes I have against me?"

Mitzi raises her hand. "Because you're intense with a terrible attitude with the public?"

I'm glad I'm not sipping my coffee because it would have spewed all over Daniel.

"No, and thanks for that, Mitzi." He sighs. "I'm a male in a female dominated industry as far as the Adirondacks go. We live in an isolated part of the state, especially when winter arrives. I plan to open a shop in a tourist area, so I have to earn a client list that will keep me going all year long. And, my dad's a doctor. This wasn't on his list of dreams come true when I announced my plan to do this."

The room is suddenly quiet.

Sandy shifts in her chair, her leather squeaking as she moves. "Dude. That's rough. Why are you putting yourself through it?"

Another sigh. "Hair is like art to me. Stereotypes aside, my grandma did hair, and I enjoyed watching her create magic. I love Lake George and I want to do this. Although I can't help people with medicine like my dad, I hope I can by giving them confidence."

His intensity makes sense.

Claire flips that blonde hair of hers. "I can relate to some of what you say. You're good, Daniel. You'll be just fine. Me? I'm average, if that. I could read the book all day long and I'd still be a mess at this. But I want to keep my mom's legacy alive." Claire's natural beauty makes it difficult to take her seriously, but she has our attention. "Anyway, funny what brought us here. Sandy, how about you?"

"It's the lure of scissors, isn't it?" Daniel smirks.

Sandy, with her dark clothes, hair, and makeup, looks like she could jump up and throttle him. "You're hysterical. You know what? I'm not so different than the rest of you. I think of all of this like art, too. With all my tats and piercings I get that I won't fit into every work environment, and I don't want to. I think I could rock a kid haircut or a mom perm. Carla? Your turn. Why cosmetology? Personally, I think your sheriff job was much more interesting."

I remember way too many nights on duty when a babysitter was taking care of Noah. Domestic abuse calls. Drunken arguments to break up around the county. No thanks.

"It wasn't as glamorous as you think, Sandy. For me, law enforcement paid the bills. My dad was a cop and when I became a teen mom, I was willing to do whatever it took to not have him disappointed in me." I look to the ground so I don't have to look at anyone or their reactions. "They paid for my training, and that was my career. But I always looked forward to friends asking me to trim their bangs or color their hair. Last year an elderly man who believed in me left some of his inheritance to me and stated I needed to use it for this, and to help me open a shop. So, here I am."

I glance around but can't tell from their faces what they're thinking.

"That has to be the most amazing story I've ever heard. You should write a book." Claire says.

Right. The teen mom who leaves the sheriff's office to cut hair, all while waffling between two men. There's a book people will rush to read.

"You're too kind. But I don't think my story is that interesting."

Ella rushes through the class door with a minute to spare.

"Hey, Ella. We're talking about why we applied here. How come you want to be a stylist?" Mitzi asks, just as Rose enters the room and stands at the lectern.

Ella's black eye isn't as visible as when I discovered it, but she appears as harried as she had that day. "Freedom. Becoming a stylist is my ticket to freedom."

⧗⧗⧗

Rose spends the entire day introducing us to the different types of haircutting implements. After she displays regular haircutting scissors, thinning shears, razors with safety guards, and then hair clippers, combs, and clippies, she asks us to join her at a circular table.

"I have pictures of haircuts from magazines. Let's go through one implement after another and find pictures you think best match what was used to accomplish the style you see." Rose glances around the table. "Ready? This should be easy. Find a picture that looks like regular scissors were used. Go." She smiles as we scramble for a magazine and start leafing through the pictures.

Ella finds one first, followed by Daniel. Then me.

"Great work. Okay, how about this one. A razored look."

This time Sandy beats us to the find. Daniel and I trail behind with our displays.

No matter what combination Rose asks for, Daniel and I are neck-and-neck. Speaking of neck, his is turning crimson.

"Competition getting to you?" I tease him.

"Honestly, yes. I looked at the examples in the book until my eyes crossed. I know these."

Rose laughs. "Okay. I think you're all familiar with the implements. Now, it's time to learn how to use them."

"Great. We get to use the heads and start cutting." Mitzi was ready to spring from her chair.

Rose waves her index finger back and forth. "Not so fast, Miss Davis."

Daniel sits taller in his seat. "We haven't covered four and five section parting."

Another smile from the teacher. "Right. Nor have I talked about texturizing, shingling, or tapering."

Claire raises her hand. "Or thinning the hair."

Daniel groans. "That's texturizing."

The blonde narrows her eyes. "You know, it's not going to do you much good when you have the book memorized yet have no clients because you're so infuriating."

A chorus of "yeah's" rise up and I watch Claire sit taller.

⧗⧗⧗

I use the lunch break to walk around town and clear my head. I can't shake the lost puppy look Wayne had when Will told him the two of us were planning a future. The sermon on Esther and Brooke's prayer also vies for my attention.

"Penny for your thoughts."

My focus was on power walking and thinking, not on anyone around me. As soon as I look up, Daniel walks past me before stopping.

I turn around and join him. "You wouldn't need a salon, Daniel. I have so many thoughts you could retire a wealthy man."

"You seem pretty clear-headed to me. Sure gave me a run for my money with those magazines."

I shrug. "I spent a lot of lonely nights combing through celebrity magazines gazing at their hair." Memories of Noah as a toddler, asleep after dinner, come to mind. No Will or Wayne in the picture back then.

"It's served you well, Carla. Say, can I ask you something?"

I take my phone out of my pocket and peek at the time. The afternoon session's ready to start in ten minutes. I gesture Daniel to follow me.

"I guess."

"Am I as obnoxious as Claire says I am?"

Oh boy. He's belittled my hair. My clothes. My work at school. But, he also helped me when Noah was at the hospital.

"You've shared why you're so driven, so I understand."

He chuckles. "That's a polite way to agree with Claire."

"You're a bit intense. I think if you loosen up, you won't come across as harsh."

As we reach the building, he opens the door for me. "Care to be my accountability partner? Kindly let me know when I'm crossing a line?"

I don't think I have that kind of time.

"Will you help us girls if we're having trouble?"

Daniel lets out a dramatic sigh. "That's asking a lot. Honestly, as an accountability partner, the only one I thought I'd help was you."

Me? I'm so over my head on so many levels. If Daniel knew, he'd withdraw his offer.

⧖⧖⧖

Betty's warm smile is a welcome sight when I walk through the front door mid-week.

"You've been a stranger lately, Carla. Is school really that busy?" Her pink track suit swooshes as she walks over to the dining table to arrange the plates.

I hang my coat and shake off my boots. It reminds me of Will doing the same at my house, always ready to ask me about my day. "Yes. We're in haircutting now. There's so many terms to learn. I'm going to make flashcards after dinner. We're practicing on the heads and it won't be long before we're out on the floor with real clients that will be coming to us. It's enough to bring on an anxiety attack." I try to laugh, but the stress is too palpable.

Grabbing the milk from the fridge, she pours the drink into a big glass. "I'm sure you're doing fine, dear. I made chicken and biscuits. Thought that would be a nice comfort meal for this cold winter evening. Perhaps later I can help you study?"

I glance over at the diminutive senior citizen. "Oh, Betty. That's not a very exciting evening for you."

"Neither is watching mysteries on TV all night."

"I can study with Daniel. He asked if I'd be his partner. So you don't have to help me if you don't want to." I don't want to obligate her, but she seems willing.

Betty chuckles. "I don't mind at all. Although, I'm curious. Why did you agree to Daniel as your partner? I thought he wasn't very nice." She gestures for me to join her at the table.

We sit and I hand her a bowl of green peas. "He's a bit competitive, but he's coming around. The whole class is kind of getting to know each other better and working together. Daniel seems genuine in wanting to help out."

Betty shakes her head. "I can't keep up. You have your man friend. Then, Noah's dad. And now, this Daniel."

Before I scoop the chicken onto my plate, I pause. "You make my life sound like a soap opera. I promise, Daniel's just a colleague."

She folds her hands. "Ready to pray? It sounds like there's a lot to take to God besides being thankful for our meal."

Is my life really as chaotic as Betty sees it?

⧗⧗⧗

It's a two-cup-of-coffee morning before I take my place in the practice salon. I bite my lip to stop a yawn as I look across the array of scissors spread out at my station. Daniel stops at the station to my right, his own Gloversville Beauty School mug in hand.

"I'm not ready for this. I stayed up past one looking at my notes." He sips and puts the cup down.

"I made flash cards and studied until I fell asleep."

Rose claps her hands five minutes later. All of us look up and notice her smile.

"It's time to discover how well you know your haircutting instruments and parting skills. I'm going to visit each station and hand you a card. I'm looking for each of you to choose the right implement, perform the right part, and start the cut. No one has the same card, so don't look to a neighbor. You either know it, or you don't." She keeps her smile, but I feel a chill all the same. "Oh, and I'm looking for everything leading up to and including the scissor selection. Use your bacterial information and basic setup we learned in previous units. You will be graded for accuracy."

I glance at Ella, but she appears focused on the array of scissors.

"Okay, I'll start with Claire." Rose announces, walking to Claire's station.

"Oh, man."

We chuckle as soon as we hear Claire's grumble. Once Rose leaves her work space, she weaves back and forth to the others, leaving me as the last to receive a card.

"Ready, Carla?" The owner and instructor offers a warm smile as she hands me a piece of paper.

I flip it over and look.

Give your mannequin a 5 section part and prepare to texturize.

"Yes."

"Good. I'll be back."

Once I prep my station, I reach for the clippies and thinning shears. My hands shake, so I take a deep breath and pray. "Okay, God. This is a simple task for You. It isn't even a big deal for everything going on here. I'm nervous, and I need Your help. Help me focus. Give me Your strength. Amen."

While Rose works through Claire, Daniel, and Mitzi, I complete the part and have thinning shears in hand. When the instructor approaches me, I feel steady.

"Good parting. Okay, I'd like you to start to texturize. Don't talk me through it, I already know your reasoning and whether it's correct. Just do."

And I'm back to feeling nervous.

Five minutes later, Rose raises her hand. "That's enough, Carla. You did it exactly as I wanted to see. Excellent." She walks away, and Ella's right behind her.

"Congrats, Carla. Great job." Ella starts toward me, but I'm so excited, I skip over to her.

"Thanks. How did you do?"

The raven-haired woman I want to get to know better offers a small smile. "She said I'm on the fast track to be a leading stylist wherever I want. I really needed the boost."

Rose claps to get our attention, so Ella waves and returns to her station. I head back to mine, but Daniel and I are heading toward each other. As we both dance around each other to reach our stations, he slips on the hair from my manikin I never swept up. He falls on his backside.

"Daniel. Are you okay?" I extend my hand but his eyes narrow and he moves to a standing position by himself.

"There's nothing excellent about a stylist who is a hazard to her clients and colleagues."

Rose clears her throat. "Daniel's correct. I'm sure this was an oversight, but a real client would probably sue you." She sighs. "And win."

With all eyes on me, I quickly sweep the hair, take my seat and look to the floor. And when I feel the staring is over, I brush away my tears.

⧖⧖⧖

After lunch, Les introduces thermal hairstyling. I can't help looking outside to watch the snow fall. February snows are nothing new, but I'm too tired to pay extra attention. Oh, to be back at Betty's stretched out on her recliner.

Imagine my surprise when at dismissal it isn't snowplows I see, but two men.

Wayne, and a man I don't recognize.

But Ella does.

"Jimmy. What're you doing here? I promised you I'd come right home." She doesn't even have her coat on, and he's already inside standing next to her.

"They're calling for all kinds of snow. I thought I'd get you first, then we'd swing by and get the kids. The roads are terrible."

She picks up her briefcase and stuffs papers in every which way. "Okay, but the buses are probably the safest place for the kids to be."

The man with brooding eyes shoots Ella a look that I've seen countless times. When I arrested men for domestic abuse.

"Ella, I'm not going to argue with you. I insist we leave together."

She doesn't even say goodbye or glance at us as she rushes out, the bully gripping her by the crook of her arm.

I'm grateful Wayne waits for me to gesture him to enter and he passes Ella on his way in. He raises his eyebrows while I shake my head.

"What brings you by? We aren't doing live cuts yet."

88

"I didn't know if you knew how bad it is out there. I thought I'd take you home, if you wanted." That smile that got us both in a heap of trouble back in high school is as charming today.

"Thanks, but I don't have far to go. Did you check in with Noah to make sure he got home safe?"

"No. You dismiss before they do. I figured you'd call Will later and check in."

Right. I should. Another goof today.

"I will. If it makes you feel better, you can follow me to make sure I get back to Betty's without problems."

He nods, a slight smirk also opens up.

"What? I didn't say anything funny."

"No. Ironic. I think there are a few men in your life who follow you around to make sure you're okay. I wonder how long they'll keep it up."

As Wayne finishes his sentence, I feel like I've been punched in the gut. He's right, but it's not funny. Who will walk beside me in life, instead of following?

Chapter Eleven

It's not the smell of bacon but the sound of Jenna's sobs that wakes me Saturday morning. Once I sit up, I see she's on the edge of my bed, tissues in hand.

"I hope it's okay. Noah said you wouldn't mind if I came in."

I kick off the sheets and rub my eyes. "No problem. What's going on?"

She takes a deep breath and blows into her tissue. "The wedding. I don't think it's going to work."

Jenna's not a drama queen. Sassy, yes, but for her to be this upset is unusual.

"What isn't working? You and Ben?"

"The plans. Mom said we need to postpone. And she's right, it's less than two months away."

I nod. "Okay. What does Ben think?"

She hiccups another cry. "He made it clear he doesn't want to wait another minute."

I resist smiling because I can see Ben saying that. I move closer to her and pat her knee. "Here's the big question. What do you want? How much is there to do for the wedding you want?"

I pray her answer doesn't include a bridal shower right away because that hasn't even been on my radar, and that makes *me* want to cry.

She looks at me. "I just want to marry Ben. I don't care about the details. I even offered to find a judge. He told me one day I'd regret it. But Mom insists on having a professional photographer and fancy cake and..."

I raise my hand. "Who's paying for your wedding?"

"Ben and me." Her voice is soft.

"Then it seems like the two of you should be in charge of your wedding. Do you want to make a list of what needs to be accomplished and who can help? See if there's enough time to get it all done?"

She blows into the tissue. "Carla, thank you. If this were an event at the senior center, I'd have a clear head. But, I guess because it's my wedding, I can't make sense of it. Are you sure you have time?"

I glance at the clock on my dresser. Will wants to go to the Saratoga Springs mall, but there's plenty of time. He'll understand. He always does.

"Don't worry. Let me get my tablet and I'll take notes."

An hour later, Jenna and I finish her list and she calls Ben.

"You're okay with Memorial Day weekend? I know I said April but I need a little more time. You think he'll do the invitations? That helps so much, Ben. You're the best. I promise. I'll be yours soon. I love you." With a giggle, she clicks off and faces me.

"It's done. Memorial Day is still spring. It's not that far off and gives us time to ask Janice Beebe if she'll make a cake for us. Pastor Craig's oldest will be done with college by then, and he's a good photographer. Ben says the editor at the weekly is a whiz with printing and will do invitations. This is happening, Carla. Thanks to you."

"I promise to put a fun shower together for you, too." In the middle of school, commuting, parenting and figuring out what to do with Wayne.

Jenna jumps up for a hug. "I know how busy you are. It's not a big deal."

A shower is an important part of the wedding plans even though I don't feel very competent. "How about if I'm overwhelmed, I call Shirley. She's your right hand woman at the center. I know she'd be a great help if I need her."

"Call her. She's amazing. Speaking of phoning, I still have to talk to my family in Ohio."

I don't envy that conversation. "I'll be praying."

She starts for the hallway but stops. "Carla, I hope you and Will have as much happiness as Ben and me. You guys totally deserve it."

⧗⧗⧗

Before we can head to the mall, Will and I go to JB's to pick up Noah from work. As soon as Will pulls into the plaza lot, Wayne's paramedic SUV comes into view. My stomach tightens as we park next to the vehicle.

"Did you know he'd be here?" Will glances at me as he turns off the ignition.

"No. He's probably getting something to eat between calls."

Will nods but doesn't reply.

We walk into the store and find Noah at the register waiting on his dad. Noah spots us first.

"Hey Mom, Will. I'm almost done. I'll finish with Dad's groceries and then I'll let Ben know I'm ready to go."

I join them at the bagging area and grab a plastic bag to help out while Will stands close by.

"Hey Carla, thanks for letting me follow you to your rental this week." Wayne smiles and retrieves his wallet from his back pocket.

Noah keeps scanning items, but glances at me.

Will coughs. "What is this about Wayne going to your place?"

A nervous laugh escapes. "He didn't, not really. It was the night of that surprise storm. He followed me to Betty's to make sure I arrived safely."

Wayne nods. "Good thing. On my way back my scanner started going crazy. There were a few accidents. Glad you weren't one of them."

I finish packing the groceries and slide them over to Wayne. This conversation needs to end quickly.

"You know, Carla was a sheriff. She's got plenty of driving experience." Will moves next to my side and puts his arm around my shoulder.

Wayne sighs. "I know that."

His tone sounds as short as his reply.

"I didn't want to assume she was okay. It was important to me that I make sure she was safe. I think it says a lot about someone when they go the extra mile."

Noah glances at his father. "Forty-two dollars and twenty-eight cents. We still having lunch tomorrow, Dad?"

Wayne hands him cash. "Absolutely. Looking forward to it." He turns to me. "Thanks for bagging my groceries. Will, always a pleasure."

Wayne exits as we wait on Noah to let Ben know he's leaving. Will drops his arm to his side as soon as Wayne's out of sight. "Carla, you two have history and he's Noah's father. But I'm starting to resent the guy. If I didn't know better, I'd say Wayne's trying to win you back. And I don't like it."

⧗⧗⧗

It takes nearly the entire seventy-mile trip before Will returns to his laid back self. We exit the truck and enter the food court, where Noah makes a beeline for the pretzel place.

"What about you? Anything special you want to eat or shop for?"

As I look into Will's kind eyes I realize how much his gaze exudes warmth. "No, you decide. I'm glad to be here." I squeeze his hand.

He returns the gesture. "Really? Thanks, honey. I was worried maybe I let you down."

Will leads us to the taco line.

"I don't understand."

He faces me. "Listening to Wayne, he sounds like your hero. He shows up at the right time and says all the perfect things. And then there's me. The most exciting thing I offer you is a trip to the mall."

Even though the line moves forward, I stay still. "Will Marshall, I'm not looking for excitement. I think I've had enough of that for a lifetime between my old job and being a teen mom." A rush of emotions slam into my throat as I try to get the words out, my confusion between the two dissipating. "You've taken care of Noah, leaving your own house to stay in mine while I'm away. You have no idea what that means to me. I can't think of anyone who would make such a sacrifice. I know for a fact Wayne wouldn't."

"How can you be so sure?"

I blink back tears. "Because he walked away the second I told him I was pregnant in high school."

Will clears his throat and wipes his eye with his sleeve as we move ahead in the line, neither of us saying anything for a while. When it's our turn, he gestures for me to go first.

Once I order my taco salad, I step aside so Will can speak. It hits me as he does that I need to talk to Wayne, and soon. My phone rings, and I take it out of my purse and shrug as Will looks on.

"Hello?"

Daniel's voice booms through my cell phone. "Turn around."

"What?"

"Just turn around. You'll see."

I sigh and obey. There's Daniel, with Claire, Mitzi, and Sandy, smiling and waving.

I disconnect the call and throw the cell back in my purse as I gesture for Will to follow me. "What are you guys doing here?"

Mitzi speaks first. "Blowing off some steam. Claire thought of it."

I nod and touch Will's arm as I introduce my friends.

Will chuckles. "Ah, the beauty school gang."

Daniel offers his hand. "I hope Carla's sharing good things."

Will looks to me and I shrug.

Claire giggles. "Daniel, the perm fumes must've gotten to you. You know we've all gone home venting about you."

Daniel nods. "I suppose I deserve that. What are you guys doing?"

"I had to get some clothes for work and thought we'd go to Sears. Carla's son is here somewhere." Will glances around the storefronts.

"You two probably don't want to shop with us. I know you don't get a lot of time alone." Sandy's smile is flat to match her Goth look, despite her kind gesture.

"That's true. You guys see her more than I do these days. But that's okay. Once Carla graduates and gets her license, she'll be back in Speculator Falls with her own shop. It'll all be worth it." He squeezes my hand and doesn't let go.

Mitzi looks to the others. "They're so adorable."

"I suppose. If you care about that sort of thing." Daniel deadpans.

Claire rolls her eyes and reaches for his elbow. "C'mon, killjoy. Let's leave them be."

After saying goodbye, the group heads to the food court and Will and I amble toward Sears.

"We're like a little family," I tell him.

"Even Daniel?"

"Sure. We're all trying to do well and graduate. We compete and bicker, but we're rooting for each other, too. He's like the annoying, over-achieving brother."

Will smiles. "Gotcha. Brother. That works."

My eyebrows form a "V." "You okay?"

He reaches down and plants a kiss on my cheek. "Yep. I let my mind get the best of me. Sometimes I worry that you might dump me for someone else. Stupid, right?"

I shudder thinking about the call I have to make to Wayne.

As I pick up my order, I know my mind is set. I don't plan to ever tell Will.

⧗ ⧗ ⧗

A waft of hyacinth dances by as I enter school and find Brandi looking like spring in her canary yellow blouse.

"Ready for wet cuts today, Carla?"

I walk over to the table with our customized mugs and reach for mine, filling it with coffee. "I think so. I studied the material, but the hands-on practice will be more telling."

Brandi smiles. "You'll do fine. Rose asked me to print out grades up to the beginning of April, and yours is right here." She waves a piece of paper. "You're on track to graduate with distinction."

I can't get to the front desk fast enough. Holding onto the printout, I stare at the letters. I'm doing well. If only I could be as successful with communication as I am with hair. I have to call Wayne and tell him there's no future between us beyond caring for Noah.

But I keep procrastinating.

"Good morning, Carla. Did you get your grades?" Mitzi greets me as I walk upstairs to the classroom.

"I did. How are you doing for the not-quite-half-way mark?"

Her smile reveals what looks like newly-whitened teeth. "Great. A minus."

We head inside the room where Daniel, Ella, Claire and Sandy are seated.

"How'd you do?" Daniel's gaze rests on me.

"I'm passing." And suspecting he wants to "one-up" me with grades.

Ella and Sandy exchange smiles.

"What grade?" he continues.

I sigh. "An A. Happy?"

Daniel starts to respond when a noise erupts from the back. We turn and find Claire in tears, blowing her nose.

"What's wrong?" Mitzi asks.

Daniel jogs over and hands Claire a fresh tissue. "You okay?"

She blows again. "My grades are terrible. I want to do well to honor my mom, but I'm not even close." She slides her printout to Daniel, who flips it over.

His eyes widen a little, but he doesn't say anything.

"I'm not a great test taker. I get nervous when we work in the lab. But I want to do this." Claire sniffles, but still looks as if she could model at a moment's notice and be the most gorgeous one on the catwalk.

"We could help you." Ella offers, joining the small circle gathering at Claire's table.

"Right. Sandy's a natural when it comes to the textbook. She's helped me a lot." Mitzi looks to her friend, who continues.

"Carla's a whiz with the heads. We could get some extras and practice."

I nod. "I'd love to help. Claire, you can do this."

Daniel folds his arms across his chest. "What about me? I have the same grades as Carla."

Claire rolls her eyes. "I don't want to be a pawn in a game."

Mitzi sighs. "Really, Daniel. Have some compassion."

He clears his throat. "No, you don't get it. I feel left out here. I want to help." He faces the blonde beauty. "I promise, I won't be uptight or compare grades with anyone. I guess that's just me being insecure, trying to measure up. I don't get a lot of fanfare with the family for going into the hair business when my dad's a doctor."

Claire looks up and gives a faint smile. "Okay. You guys are the best. Thank you."

We head back to our chairs when I pass Daniel. "Was that for real?"

"What? My confession to Claire?" he whispers.

I nod. "Do you really feel insecure?" *I thought that was just me---the teen mom handed this dream and feeling completely unworthy.*

"Try attending dinner parties with the folks when their friends ask what line of work you're in. Explaining I want to open a salon in Lake George is a surefire way to erase those pasted on smiles they all wear."

"Wow. I've been pretty hard on you. I'm sorry if I made things worse."

He chuckles. "It's fine. I think we both challenge each other, and that's not bad. You remind me this is worth fighting for. Because..." He winks. "I do plan to graduate as head of the class."

⌛⌛⌛

Between extra hours helping Claire, my own studying, preparing for Jenna's bridal shower, and entertaining Betty with casual conversation after school each evening, I still haven't called Wayne. I decide after school Thursday I have to talk to him. After I go for a run.

"Carla, do you have plans this evening? I don't feel like making dinner and I thought I'd treat you. You've been working so hard, dear." Betty barely allows me inside before greeting me. I need Jenna to meet her. Betty would be such an asset to the senior center when able to travel to it.

"I thought I'd go for a jog, then I have some work to do."

Her aqua eyes seem to dull to a sad gray. "Oh. Well, never mind. It was just a thought."

I drop my purse on the table. "It's a good idea. Let me get my exercise in, and then we can go. Does that work?"

Her Sinatra blue eyes are back. "Wonderful." She claps.

The run gives me time to think and pray. There's so much going through my mind between Noah, school, Will, Wayne, Jenna, and Claire. I'm not sure why Jenna listens to my advice because I feel totally inadequate.

"It's me again, Lord. The one who goofs up and is scared of doing it again. The one with a 'baby daddy' and a boyfriend. The one with a teen son who seems interested in girls and I'm not ready for that." My feet hit the pavement with purpose. "I don't know what to do with my fear. My failure." I chuckle. "My fear of failure."

Give it to The One.

I pick up the pace, wanting to be sure I'm truly hearing from the Lord. When I get the same answer more than once, I know. And that statement comes back to me even as I finish up and prepare to go out with Betty.

An hour later I find Betty with her purse, ready to go.

"Oh, Betty. I'm a sweaty mess. Can I take a few minutes to shower? You'll thank me later."

She bats her hand at the air. "Nonsense. You're fine. We're not going anywhere special. You can shower later." She opens the door and heads outside.

Well, okay then.

We end up at the local café, and I'm glad I ran before eating. I order a cheeseburger, Noah's favorite meal.

"What are you getting, Betty?"

She doesn't even pick up the menu. "I always get the BLT. Nothing better than a good sandwich at a place like this."

I look at my landlady and realize she isn't that old. If she were at Jenna's senior center, she'd be the belle of the place. "Do you get out during the week?"

"I get groceries. Go to the post office. Things like that."

"Do you sew or work on puzzles or anything crafty?"

Betty inspects the utensils. "What's this about?" She starts to rub on the top of her spoon.

"You're a beautiful woman with a lot to offer. You could volunteer or join a club or be a part of a senior center. They could use your energy. Have you ever thought about it?"

She puts the spoon on her napkin. "Not for long. I tried to go out with friends once. Did you know that when you're a widow the other women think you're after their husbands? It was the furthest thing from my mind, but it's their fear. I decided staying home's easier."

I never thought about widowed life. Then again, I haven't exactly entertained married life either.

"My best friend will be meeting with me next week for final touches on her wedding shower. Jenna's the director of the senior center in Speculator Falls. She can give you some guidance. You have so much to offer people, Betty."

"It does get pretty boring." Betty smiles.

"Well, let's change that. Life's too short to stay still and watch everyone else have fun."

A woodsy cologne aroma grabs my attention and I look up, expecting the waiter.

"Someone mention fun? I know a guy who's a ton of entertainment and doesn't wear plaid and flannel every day." Wayne's smirk ruins my appetite.

Betty smiles. "Do you know this handsome young man?"

I groan, wishing I'd made that call weeks ago. Like in high school, Wayne's hard to resist in a uniform.

"Hello. I'm Wayne Peterson, paramedic. I also happen to be Carla's first and dare I say, only love." He shakes Betty's hand and reaches for a chair behind us. "Mind if I join you pretty ladies?"

Chapter Twelve

Wayne inches his chair up to the table. "I'm on break. Had a transport from Piseco. ATV accident."

Betty gasps. "Oh, dear. Will they make it?"

Wayne nods. "I think so. Helmet saved him. Teen." He looks to me. "They think they're invincible."

Is he thinking of us years ago, or our own teen?

Betty's sweet voice breaks our gaze. "I'm Betty, by the way. Carla stays with me during the week. Wayne, what can I get you? Dinner's on me tonight."

His eyes sparkle. "Thank you, Betty. That's very kind. Cheeseburger."

She chuckles. "Funny. That's what Carla ordered."

The two banter through the meal. Each time there's a pause I want to jump in and ask Wayne to meet privately. My need to tell him the truth about our romantic future grows with each bite we enjoy.

"Carla, you're quiet this evening. Everything okay?" He leans closer.

I swallow hard. "Actually, I need to talk to you. Perhaps you can drive me back to Betty's." I glance at her. "If you don't mind."

She waves us off. "You two have fun."

His smile widens. "Sounds great. My schedule's flexible unless there's a call."

Please don't let there be an emergency. This conversation has to happen.

⧗⧗⧗

Once we walk Betty to her car and watch her leave, Wayne turns to me. "Did you want to walk or chat in the SUV?"

Flashes of too many times alone in his car come to mind. "Walking is good."

I zip my jacket and stuff my hands in my pockets, hoping I can pull out some courage.

"What's up? Are you worried about Noah? He's doing fine."

We walk down North Main Street without speaking for a few moments. Despite his arrogance and how he mocks Will, I can't look Wayne in the eye.

"Carla, you're the one that asked me here. What's going on?" He sighs and kicks a pebble down the sidewalk.

"I'm having trouble putting the words together." I squeak out the words before choking out a sob.

He reaches for my hand, but I jerk it back like we're playing "Hot Potato." "Maybe because you aren't supposed to say them."

I take a risk and look at his ebony hair. The chiseled chin. All the things that drove me to his arms in the first place. Qualities Noah inherited from him. "I'm so sure of what I want to say, and then I see you and the words don't come."

"I know you're confused. And I've kind of been a jerk about it. But here's what I know to be true. My feelings for you are real."

I shudder as soon as he confesses. "Sometimes that's not enough."

He nods. "True. Here's what else is true between us---we have Noah. That's something Will won't ever have in common with you. I know he's a good guy. I get that I made mistakes. But Carla, we have Noah." His words are an impassioned plea more than a statement.

I stop and wipe moisture from the corner of my eye. "I don't know."

He gives a quick squeeze to my shoulder and the touch feels like a thousand volts of electricity. "Then don't decide yet. Pray about it. I'm not going anywhere. I promise."

We turn around and head back. I want to think of Will and the wonderful things he's done, but my imagination is a blank space as Wayne and I walk in the snow.

"I can't promise my answer will be what you want to hear. Will's so good to me. And to Noah."

Wayne remains silent as he stuffs his hands in his pockets and keeps pace with me until we reach the medical SUV. It's still quiet as he drives me back to Betty's.

102

Once we arrive, he jumps out and opens the door for me as I slide out.

"Goodnight." He reaches out to me with an outstretched arm but then let the gesture fall to his side.

Safe inside the house, I close my eyes and blow out a hot breath of frustration. Because after walking with Wayne, I can't make any promises that don't seem to come from a place that believes Wayne and I were once really good together.

⧗⧗⧗

The next morning Betty greets me with a gasp. "Oh, Carla. I fell asleep before you returned. You had a phone call."

I put Betty's homemade blueberry muffin on a napkin. "Really? Who called? Why didn't they try my cell?"

She walked over to the counter and picked up my phone. "You never took it to dinner. It was your young man."

My mind scrambles faster than the eggs Betty's making. She means Will, right?

"Will? Did he say what he wanted? Is it Noah?"

Betty shrugs and hands me the device. "It didn't sound like an emergency. He wanted you to call him back. I'm sorry I didn't get the message to you earlier."

I gesture that it's no problem as I punch in the familiar numbers. Before I can say anything more to Betty, Will picks up on the first ring.

"Carla? Are you okay?"

"I'm sorry, I left my phone at Betty's and got back late." I wave to Betty and head back to my room.

His sigh comes through pretty clear. "Thank God. I was ready to call and get a sub driver so I could drive down and check on you. I was pretty worried."

"I'm fine. Betty and I went out and I forgot to take my phone." I reach for my backpack and car keys, needing to prepare for school.

"Right." He stretches the word out for a few syllables. "How come Betty was home answering her landline if you two were out?"

I tuck the phone under my chin as I pull back my hair into a pony tail. "Oh, that. We ran into Wayne. I needed to talk to him so he drove me back so Betty could go home." *Please don't ask for details.*

Another sigh. This one doesn't sound like relief. "Really. What were you talking about? Anything important?"

I look above and shut my eyes. "Of course. Wayne and I are parents. All our talks are important."

"So it was about Noah?"

This time I'm the one with a sigh. A quiet one as I venture into territory I never thought I would. "Yep. Small talk about Noah. That was the gist of it. So, can I call later? I need to get going."

"Sure thing, Honey. I'm glad you're okay. I love you."

My   temples   start   to   pulsate.   "Love   you,   too."

Chapter Thirteen

Betty giggles as I start the truck. "I can't believe I'm going on a road trip. I'm so excited."

I glance over at her and smile. As stressful as the first months of school have been, without the experience I wouldn't have friends like Ella, Mitzi, Sandy, and Claire. Even Daniel has simmered down now that he understands we're all insecure about failing and that we want to work together, not against each other. But Betty has been so much more than a landlord. She has been a blessing. Taking her back with me to Speculator Falls for a long Easter weekend feels right. And, she's happy to help me plan Jenna's shower.

"I think you're going to enjoy staying in Speculator Falls for the weekend. You'll love everyone." An image of the unnerving Kyle Swarthmore and his endless ulterior motives to befriend us in order to buy away our property comes to mind. "Well, almost everyone." I grin.

"And I won't be in the way?"

"Absolutely not. My house isn't huge, but it has three bedrooms. If you don't mind the chaos that comes with having a teen around, you'll be set for the weekend. We have a busy agenda anyway. We'll hardly be home."

I head north and feel a few love taps on my hand. "Carla, thank you. Since James died, I've been so lonely. I didn't know how much until you came into my life. We didn't have kids. All I have is my sister. It's going to be a wonderful Easter. I can just feel it." Betty lets out a dreamy sigh and looks out the window.

As I think about planning Jenna's shower, studying hair color implements and rules, spending time with Noah, dodging Wayne and making sure Will doesn't find out Wayne has feelings for me---all while celebrating Easter, I'm ready to pull over and let Betty drive while I take a nap.

⧗⧗⧗

Will and Noah elbow each other out the door as they run to the driveway to greet us. Seeing Will in a kelly-green T shirt stirs unpredictable emotions I've forgotten I've had. Refusing to turn Wayne away once and for all and lying to Will about it will do that, I suppose.

"Hey, Carla. I'm so happy we have a holiday weekend to enjoy." Will pecks a chaste kiss on my cheek, probably for Betty's sake.

"You guys remember Betty. Betty, Will and my son, Noah."

Betty shakes their hands. "You boys have a wonderful lady here."

"No argument there." Will smiles.

Noah walks to the back and unbuckles the truck liner where our suitcases are. "What time are you meeting Miss Shirley at Jack Frosty's? Can I go? Brittany, Josh and Amber are going there for ice cream." He lifts our luggage and places it on the ground as he looks at me.

I realize if I say yes, Will's left alone. "Will, I know my meeting is kind of girlie but did you want to come with? Maybe we can linger and have some ice cream, too. Frosty's will be closed tomorrow for Good Friday."

His eyes light up. "I'd love to go with you ladies. C'mon Noah, let's bring their stuff in the house and we'll get going." He grabs a suitcase and gives me another kiss as he walks by.

Betty claps her hands. "I knew this was going to be a great weekend."

⧗⧗⧗

It's dusk when we sit at the booth with Jenna's senior volunteer receptionist, Shirley McIlwain. Jenna gets the giggles when she describes Shirley's glasses and now that we're up close, I fight the temptation to smirk. Her lenses are thick and magnify her pupils. It's pretty startling if you're not used to it. When I glance at Betty, she doesn't seem to notice. She plops in the booth and says hello.

"I'm Betty. I live in Gloversville and Carla's been living with me while she's at school."

Shirley nods. "I remember Jenna mentioning you. Welcome. Will, sorry Carla dragged you here." She chuckles.

Will stretches his arm across the top of the booth and I'm very aware of how close he is. Like *The Tell Tale Heart*, when his hand rests on my shoulder, I nearly jump.

He chuckles and faces Shirley. "I'm happy to be here. Not sure how much help I can be, but Jenna's the best. If I can present a good idea or two, great." He turns to me. "You okay? You seem startled."

A high-pitched laugh fills the air and I realize the voice is mine. "No, I'm fine. I want to plan an amazing shower for Jenna. She does so much for all of us. I want to bless her." That's the truth. About her. The startled part? Why can't I tell Will what Wayne and I really shared? Why can't I tell Wayne that beyond sharing Noah, we don't have a future?

"Hey, Carla." Shirley snaps her fingers in front of my face.

"What?" I sit up straight and attempt to focus.

"Want to make sure you're paying attention. I just suggested The Harmony Inn Restaurant. I think Darla will give us the side dining room and block it off for a good price. It includes food and clean up."

I bite my lip as I think. Jenna loves the atmosphere there, as well as the mountain views.

"I'm focused. Do you want to call and ask? I doubt we'll receive a good price if I try."

The crowd looks at me. Betty tilts her head. "Why not?"

I shrug. "I gave her a speeding ticket last year."

Shirley nods and jots something in her notebook. "Yes, I'll make that call. Can I count on you for games?" She looks right in my direction, those dark, bug eyes not even blinking.

"Absolutely."

Will flashes a smile and squeezes my shoulder.

Games? Yeah, I'm full of them.

Shirley keeps writing as she talks about favors and flowers. She lifts her head and sets her gaze past me. "Carla. Isn't that your boy over there?"

I turn to see a boy with wavy, black hair holding hands across the table with Brittany Niles. My throat starts to constrict as my brain and heart battle for control. My son is holding hands with a girl. And he didn't tell me.

"Will you excuse me a moment?" I look to Will, who hasn't moved.

"Are you sure?" He shifts his arm and gives me elbow room.

I glance over and see the two laughing with Josh and Amber, who are also holding hands.

"Yes. No. Noah never told me. He knew we'd all be at the same place."

Will nods. "I'll back you up, whatever you decide."

Looking at his kind smile, I can't believe I had any trouble choosing between him and Wayne. Once I learn what's going on in Noah's life, I need to give Wayne clear direction. Will's encouragement helps me stay seated and reduced to a small wave when Noah and I lock eyes.

"You aren't going to zone out this much when you style my hair, are you?" Shirley doesn't quite have a scowl, but she isn't smiling, either. I've not been on my game for this meeting.

"I know it's getting late, but I promise you have my undivided attention. I'll make favors. Print invitations. Whatever you need."

"Okay, let's see. Invitations. Jenna already has the newspaper willing to print them off. Can you go down and pick them up next week when you get to town?" She taps her pencil on the table.

"Well, I want to."

"What's wrong?" Betty's sweet voice joins the conversation.

"When I was sheriff I also ticketed the editor and she doesn't love me."

Shirley sighs and rolls her eyes.

"I'll do it. I make deliveries there. It's no problem." Will saves the day. Again.

Now it's my turn to hold hands.

⧗⧗⧗

It's nearly midnight when Will drives us home and heads to his house. Noah heads right for the kitchen in search of snacks when I decide to linger.

"So…did you have fun at Frosty's?"

He reaches for a bag of chips. "Yep."

Let's try another angle. "It kind of looked like Josh and Amber were a couple."

Noah nods. "Yeah. Been about a month."

Alright, he's not opening up. And I have a desperate need to know what's going on. I lean against the counter and go for it. "How about you and Brittany?"

He spins around, squeezing the bag. "I knew you saw us. It's no big deal."

"Is that why you didn't say anything?" I want to come off as nonchalant but my voice is shaky.

He shakes his hand. "I didn't mention it because there was nothing to say. The night had a double date feel to it with Josh and Amber and when they started to hold hands, I figured I'd ask. She said yes. End of story."

My heartrate escalates. Wayne's bold like that. Will Noah be as forward?

"What's next?"

He opens the chips. "I figure I'll talk to Pastor on Sunday and see if the church's open for an October wedding." His face stays expressionless for a few seconds before he walks over and nudges my arm. "Mom. I'm kidding. I like Brittany, that's no secret. But I'm not even fourteen. My goals are pretty basic."

I'm sure Wayne's were, too.

Noah eats a chip. "Besides, Dad told me to be patient. Build a friendship first. He said he did everything wrong with you and he's really sorry. He was telling me about a lady he wants to go out with and he said he's taking it slow. Sounded like good advice."

Chapter Fourteen

As a child, I never understood what was so "good" about Good Friday. Years later, it still doesn't feel like a day to celebrate. The constant drizzle doesn't help, but I dress in a sweater and jeans knowing what I have to do. Confront Wayne. With Will working, the timing works.

I just dread the conversation.

An hour later Noah's at JB's to help Ben with the Easter grocery rush and Sara picked Betty up for a Speculator Falls tour and brunch. I'm on my way to Wayne's. His vehicle is in the driveway and as I park behind it, I feel my heartbeat rush. Noah's words about Wayne and a lady taking it slow are a steady drumbeat through my aching head. Shouldn't I be relieved to put a period between us?

I give my hard sheriff's knock and Wayne opens the door as he's buttoning the top of his white paramedic shirt. Before he finishes I catch a glimpse of his bare upper chest and avert my eyes by looking into his. Even worse idea.

"Carla. What a surprise. Come in." He gestures me inside, but I stay on the porch.

"No, thanks. This will be quick."

Wayne leans on the doorframe. "Okay. Is this about Noah?" He furrows his brow.

I shake my head. "Not exactly. He was holding hands with Brittany. We were talking about it and he mentioned you gave him advice."

He nods. "Right. I am allowed to do that, right?" His words sound cautious.

"Of course. It's what he said about your strategy about taking it slow."

"What? You disagree?" He tries to smile, but it doesn't quite work.

"No, you're absolutely right and we're the poster people for what happens when you rush."

He tilts his head and a stray curl falls onto his forehead.

And I'm having a terrible time focusing. "Noah mentioned you taking things slow with a lady." I spit the words out as if I've drank sour milk.

Wayne chuckles and within seconds he's enjoying a full belly laugh.

"I don't see what's so funny. One day you're confessing your feelings for me and telling me to give you a chance. The next, I'm hearing from our son that you're with a lady, taking it slow."

Wayne stands straight and walks inside, gesturing me inside. "I don't bite. Come in so we can talk."

Without a prayer or common sense, I march behind him.

"Carla. Do you know how cute you are when you're mad?" He's back to a soft laugh, but I'm not joining in.

I stand with my hands on my hips as he chuckles away, mere feet from me.

"I can't believe I was actually confused and entertaining choosing you over Will."

He instantly sobers and takes a step forward, closing the gap between us. "The lady is you. I was talking about you."

I need a second to pick my jaw off the floor. "What?"

Another move toward me. "My impulse is to go to Will Marshall and tell him to marry you or get lost because I know what I want. I was an idiot to abandon you and Noah. I don't deserve your love but something deep inside me feels like I have to at least try."

The confusion overwhelms me. Every time I try to respond, words fail.

He looks as serious as the day I told him I was pregnant. "I don't want to go slow. I don't want to waste a moment. But things between us aren't cut and dry. So, this is where I'm at. Like it, or not."

I exhale as if I've been punched. "Wow. I don't know what to say. When I'm with Will, it's a nice, easy fit. He's good to me. He always has been."

Wayne winces.

"But you. We have history. And a son. I know you're trying. I'm confused." I bury my face in my hands but they're pried loose when Wayne takes my hands in his.

"I meant it when I said I'd go slow. I'm happy to hear at least it isn't a straight up no."

Neither of us let go but thankfully we don't interlock fingers, either.

"I should go." I am nowhere near as forceful and confident as when I knocked on the door.

He releases my hands. "Do me a favor?"

I saunter toward the door and turn. "Sure."

He follows and is so close that when I move, I step on his shoe. "Go to Marshall. Look him in the eye. And be honest with yourself. Because I think once you are, you'll know he doesn't give you half the feelings I know I do."

⧗⧗⧗

As if Jenna doesn't have enough to do, she's planned a Saturday Easter Egg hunt at the senior center for the kids around the area. Not only does she ask for an update on shower plans, she wonders if I'll come to the center and stuff eggs with candy Friday afternoon.

I want to tell her everything about the quandary I'm in but watching her with her auburn hair in a bun running between tables with plastic eggs, I can't.

As soon as she sees me, she squeals, grabs my hand that still feels hot from Wayne's touch, and leads me to a table. "I'm so glad you could help. Sara and Betty are on their way. Ben's closing the store at three and he said he'd bring Noah. Will has one more delivery and he promised to help." She doesn't even take a breath.

"How many eggs do you have?"

She points to a box that has to stand five feet tall. "Fifteen hundred."

"Jenna, we aren't giving candy to everyone in the Adirondacks. We don't even have tourists coming in yet. Just us locals."

Her enthusiasm appears to deflate. "It's the first one the center's ever done. I wanted it to be big."

I nod. "You're right. I'm sorry. Show me what you want in the eggs."

Jenna claps her hands. "I have bags and bags of chocolate. Once I get Fred and Janice settled, I'll come over and sit with you. Shirley said once you paid attention, you got a lot done planning the shower." She unwraps a candy and pops it in her mouth. "Was it hard to focus with your big, strong man sitting next to you?"

I want to scoop up all the treats and eat them on the spot.

As we stuff the eggs with candy Jenna isn't sampling, more help arrives. Once Ben walks in, Jenna's face glows. Does mine with Will? Wayne? Anyone else but Noah?

"Sweetheart, we don't have enough acreage in Speculator Falls for all these eggs." Ben peeks in the box and then gives her a quick kiss.

Noah, trailing after him, widens his eyes when he sees all the plastic. "Can we put some on the logging trails? Maybe the hunters will find them."

Ben chuckles. "In November."

Before anyone can laugh, the door opens once more and Will steps in. With Wayne's voice swimming through my mind, I jump up and greet Will with a quick hug before looking him deep in the eyes.

"Well, hello to you, too." Will jokes, giving a perfunctory kiss on the cheek. Nothing to swoon over. He walks over to the table where we're gathered and whistles as soon as he sees the plethora of eggs.

"Jenna, do you know where you want all these hidden? There are a lot."

She sighs. "I only thought big. I didn't think the details through."

Will looks around at each of us and scratches his goatee. "Can I throw out an idea?"

"Absolutely. What are you thinking?"

He pulls out a chair and sits backwards in it. "It would take all of us getting the word out and getting permission from the businesses. Offer local businesses that are open tomorrow to have eggs in a basket for

114

families that visit each store. JB's, The Department Store. Coffee shop. Jack Frosty's. You get people in to shop while kids get some eggs. There's community places, too. The church could have some hidden around the front. Same for here. The library. The health center could hide eggs in their grass. Everyone could spend a better part of a day looking for eggs and getting out and about Speculator Falls."

Jenna looks to Ben. He nods. "I'd definitely have JB's involved. I'll even make a map and get copies made for the egg hunters."

Her eyes look as bright as a disco light. "You guys, thank you. I love the idea."

Will shrugs. "I'm glad I could help. It's what anyone would do for their friends and community." He moves the chair closer to the table and starts planning the next steps with Ben. Will sees Noah sitting on the far end and gestures him to join.

As I watch Will work, I realize sometimes there's more to swoon about than dazzling kisses. And I remain confused as Will saving the day and involving Noah is as attractive to me as Wayne's touch.

Chapter Fifteen

I can hear Betty singing "Up From the Grave He Arose" through the walls as I brush my teeth Easter morning. After a late night cleaning up all the eggs in the successful community Easter Egg-stravaganza as Will coined it, Betty, Noah and I are ready to finish off the weekend with a great church service.

Once I walk into the kitchen, Betty greets me with a glazed donut. "Happy Resurrection Sunday, Carla. I bought these at the donut shop yesterday to thank you for inviting me here. I had the best time visiting places with Sara and going to the senior center for the egg hunt yesterday."

I reach for the glazed treat and enjoy a bite. It's warm, so Betty probably put it in the microwave. Even in my own home she takes great care of me. "I'm mad I didn't think of it sooner. Anytime you want to come with me to Speculator Falls, say the word. Everyone loved meeting you."

I glance at the microwave clock and notice if we're going to be on time, we need to leave. Yet Noah's not around. "Excuse me, Betty. I need to get Noah in gear."

She nods as she walks over to the donut box, probably to enjoy another while she waits.

"Noah, time to leave." I call out and knock at the same time.

He opens the door before I can get to my third knock. He's wearing a nice, albeit wrinkled shirt and khaki pants. His hair's slicked back. I wish he dressed like this every Sunday or even every holiday, but the huge basket he's holding tells me this is all about Brittany.

"Sorry. I'm ready." He balances the gift as he gestures for me to go first down the hall.

"Happy Easter. Are we not going to talk about the big rabbit in the room?" I reach for my purse and point to the chocolate bunny surrounded by five other kinds of chocolate, wrapped in cellophane.

Noah looks down at the basket and grins. "Ben helped me put it together with stuff from the store. He said girls go crazy for chocolate." He ignores the donuts and walks to the front door.

I sigh, not so sure Ben should be encouraging this romance.

⧗⧗⧗

Pastor Craig wastes no time after the choir sings and the ushers take an offering. He's passionate about his message titled "Make a Decision, Already."

This Easter message can't be about my inability to choose between two men. Can it?

"I'm going rogue with my message this morning. I know most pastors would use Christ's miraculous resurrection for their talking points. It's an amazing story that defines who I am and what I do every day." He rakes his hand through his hair. "I want to spend a few minutes talking about a member of the story who played a key role and had a horrible time making decisions. So he tried to make deals."

My shoulders relax. This can't pertain to me if it's about one of the gospels. I glance at Will, who seems to have full attention on our pastor. Will's bulletin is open to the space where we can take notes, and his pen is ready. His enthusiasm for Godly things still feels like a magnet to my weak nature.

Pastor clicks on a projector and displays an image of a man. "Pilate. He had to keep a balance with the Jews. He wasn't a fan and his history with them wasn't positive. But if he exerted his authority too much, he knew they'd get upset and he'd be in trouble. What do you do when you want to keep everyone happy?" He forwards to the next slide. It's a picture from the game show, *Let's Make a Deal.* "Pilate, even under great pressure to make a decision about Jesus, refused and instead worked on deals. Let's turn to John 18:31."

I take notes almost as fast as Will. I'm feeling pretty good about my own choices or lack of when I compare my life to my Pilate notes. The guy tries his best to avoid Jesus. Pastor makes a great point, though.

"You can't avoid a God who's everywhere and looking for you."

I peek at Noah, who sits with the other teens, including Brittany. Who I can't see because the gigantic basket blocks most of her face. Noah's staring ahead and appears to be paying attention. I think about my teen years and how I avoided anything that appeared to be religious, until I learned I was pregnant and Wayne lost interest in me faster than a game of hot potato. My parents showed me the door. There weren't any deals going on back then.

"When avoiding Christ didn't work, he looked to what everyone else would do. The culture around him." Pastor's on a roll giving us the backstory on Pilate. "And when that didn't work, Pilate tried to compromise. Killing Jesus would be too messy of a choice for him to make. But a beating? That would satisfy the people and make them go away. Now let's look at John 19:1."

Pages flip throughout the sanctuary. Once we read the passage, Pastor Craig pauses.

"Pilate wanted the crowds off his back and won't admit that Christ had any power over His Kingdom, Him, or the world. He wanted perfection, but is remembered as the guy with blood on his hands, no matter how hard he tried to wash them. Pilate should have been resolved."

Okay, I think Will is God's choice for me until I see Wayne, but at least I don't have blood on my hands. That's kind of harsh.

Pastor Craig closes his Bible and leans on the podium. "Friends, you might be thinking because you aren't in charge of life and death, you're in good shape."

Uh-oh. I don't like where this is going.

"If you walked in here today thinking it's the right thing to do on Easter to go to church, but you've never thought about the sacrifice Christ made and how you factor into it, consider this---He's already made His decision about you. And it's all about love and grace. Would you at the very least give Him some time at the altar to think about making a commitment for a relationship with Him?"

That puts me in the clear. I've done that.

Pastor Craig clears his throat. "Perhaps you have that faith but there is another decision you're facing and instead of making it, you're tossing out deals faster than Pilate."

My heartbeat feels like it's qualifying for NASCAR.

"You too are invited to come to the altar. Spend some time in prayer. Allow one of us to pray with you. Because as the great Ronald Reagan once said about a season of indecision he faced, 'I learned then if I don't make a decision, it will be made for me."

Looking around, everyone seems to nod and smile. If they feel sick and sweaty with anxiety, they aren't showing it.

I nearly sprint to the front for prayer.

Brooke stands next to her husband and the two look ready to encourage anyone going forward. When I retreat to a corner so all of Speculator Falls won't hear me confess and most likely cry, Brooke offers a kind smile and walks my way.

"Carla. Is there anything I can pray about with you today?" Her voice is as soft as cotton.

"Yes. I have a decision to make. I've been dishonest. I don't like how weak I am, but when I try to stand and do the right thing, I'm confused."

She nods and wraps an arm around me. "I see. I'm going to go ahead and pray, okay?"

"Thanks, Brooke. I'm struggling."

She closes her eyes. "Father, we come before You thanking You first for this day. For loving us so much You sent Your Son to die on the cross in our place. That He is alive and we celebrate that this Resurrection Sunday. We also thank You for Your nature. You forgive when we confess. Carla has admitted she has sinned. She's not been truthful. She's confused."

I try to close my eyes but right before I do, I see Will. He's close to the front, but at a respectful distance. He's praying. That kind of deep prayer that storms the heavens. I don't deserve such a kind man. Tears fall onto the carpet as soon as I shut my eyes.

Brooke squeezes my shoulder. "Carla's in a lot of transition this year and we ask in Your Son's name that You order her steps and direct her path. Make her way clear. Eliminate all confusion in her life. And we give You thanks for that in advance, Father. You get the glory, honor and praise in Christ's name. Amen."

I see she has watery eyes. Does she know my situation? "Thank you, Brooke."

"You're very welcome. Carla, you're an amazing woman of God. Don't ever forget that."

Forget it? I need help believing it in the first place.

⧗⧗⧗

Forty minutes later it feels like half the congregation is sitting around Ben's long dining room table as Jenna and Sara place ham slices and boiled potatoes down. Noah starts to reach for the bowl until he looks at my we're-going-to-wait face.

Will leans in close to me. "Everything okay, Sweetheart? I was a little worried about you at the altar earlier."

I look at his sage eyes for a moment, my throat catches as I get caught up in how completely adorable he is. It's much more than his enticing eyes, strong build, or handsome smile. His compassion is alluring. "It's starting to be. Will, I don't say it enough but when I looked over and saw you praying, it moved me. Dating a Godly man is a gift. Thank you for being amazing."

The room quiets as I speak and everyone hears my sentiments. I feel warmer as the crowd stares at us. My right hand reaches for Will's. He lifts it and kisses the back of my palm.

"I love you." He mouths.

I squeeze his hand. "I love you, too."

Ben clears his throat. "Well, on that sweet note, let's say grace and dig in."

Not even an hour later I take plates back to the kitchen, wishing I'd worn stretchy pants to accommodate all I ate. Ben's in there loading the dishwasher.

"Hey, Ben. Great dinner. Thanks for having us."

He straightens. "I'd love to take the credit but Grandma and Jenna did the cooking. I can't wait to marry that girl and have Jenna be in this house every day." Ben glows every time he speaks my best friend's name.

"It won't be long. After Easter is Memorial Day. You're almost there." I place two plates on the lower rack. "Say, Noah tells me you helped him put that Easter basket together for Brittany Niles."

He rinses some silverware. "Yeah. I had a great chocolate supplier this year. It was fun to help him."

"Thing is, do you think you should encourage him with this? He's a kid."

Ben looks up, his eyebrows furrow. "What? You didn't want him to give a girl some chocolate? I didn't send him to Pastor for wedding counsel." He tries to laugh, but it's more like a snort.

"I think Noah is way more interested in Brittany than she is in him. I don't want him to get hurt."

He nods and turns off the water, turning toward me. "Carla, I don't mean to offend you but Noah and I talk a lot at the store. He seems to have a good head on his shoulders. I'm sorry if I overstepped my bounds."

I close the dishwasher, glad we were able to have the conversation.

"But know this, Carla. Noah talks a lot about you, too. And his dad. The boy's convinced you and Wayne have a future because Noah says his father said as much."

I wince as the words come at me like blows to the stomach.

"And if you're worried about Noah being hurt, you better analyze your choices before you criticize others. Wasn't thirty minutes ago you declared your love for my best friend in there, and Wayne's nowhere to be seen."

Chapter Sixteen

Our long weekend off from school feels more like a month. I walk in the front door of Gloversville Beauty School trying to shake off my Speculator Falls life and remember where we're at in our cosmetology classes.

"Good morning, Carla. Did you have a nice weekend?" Brandi wears a pair of red frames that highlight her blue dress. She's so fashionable.

I stifle a yawn and fight images of Ben chastising me about Wayne. "I did. It was great to be with my son."

She takes a sip out of her GBS mug. "Teenager, right? How's that going?"

Now I'm trying to forget the memory of my little boy holding hands with Brittany. "So far, so good. It's hard not to worry. I might even say impossible. He's noticing girls and it scares me." Like, a lot.

Brandi nods. "I give you credit. I'm not sure I could be a good mom. There's so much bad news everywhere. I would be scared to bring a child into the world."

I sigh and reach for my mug and pour some coffee from the pot. "It's tempting to think negative all the time. I try to focus on the purpose I believe Noah has to make a positive difference in the world. He's a great kid. I just wish he wasn't growing up so fast." I find the liquid creamer. "Don't worry, one day you'll realize what a great mom you will be and nothing will stand in your way."

She smiles. "Okay, I'll believe you. But only because you're such an honest person."

Ben's stern face comes to mind once again.

Oh, yeah. I'm a walking model for authenticity.

After I make my drink, I head upstairs and see most of the gang is already in the classroom. Daniel and Claire are chatting, and in the opposite corner, so are Mitzi and Sandy. It looks like Ella's in the back, where I take a seat. Once I put my bag on the next seat, I see it's her. And her eyes are sunken in as if she hasn't slept in weeks.

"Hey, Ella. Everything okay?"

She bites her lip and nods. "Yeah."

I unpack the book I need and reach for a highlighter before I take a seat. "Did you have a nice Easter?"

She nods and places her arms on the desk, a dozen or so bracelets clang as she does. Although the room is almost stuffy, she's wearing a heavy navy sweater. "It was nice. Kids were crazy with sugar highs." Her voice is soft and she tries to smile but I think exhaustion rules.

Opening my notebook, I know I'm playing sheriff. "You never told me what your husband does."

Ella looks at her book and randomly flips pages. I can barely hear her. "He's between jobs."

Okay, unemployed because of economics and a layoff? Or, fired because of anger?

"I'm sorry. I'm sure it's stressful going to school and taking care of the house and kids. I have the one teenager and I know I'm exhausted a lot."

Another nod.

I reach out and give her the slightest touch on the top of her hand.

She winces.

"If you need anything, I can help."

"Thank you." Ella uses that hand to brush her eye. As the bracelets move, I see dark purple against her ivory skin.

⏳⏳⏳

By the time I drag myself into Betty's kitchen, it's after six in the evening and I feel too tired to eat. But she has a pork chop casserole on the table and her sweet smile wears my resistance to decline.

"How was your first day back, dear?"

I take a pork chop and place it on my plate. "It was hard to get back into the groove. We're still working on perms, and I think it's all I can smell." And all I can see is Ella's bruised wrist.

She reaches for the dish of green beans. "That doesn't sound fun at all."

"I can't believe in this day and age we haven't come up with a chocolate scented permanent, you know?"

We chuckle and eat in silence for a few minutes. Betty's the first to speak.

"Carla, I wanted to say once again how much I loved going with you to Speculator Falls. I had the best time with Sara. I can see why everyone loves her so."

I smile as I think about the matriarch who looks like Mrs. Claus but hugs like a wrestler. "Trust me, the feeling was mutual. Sara told me at the senior center how much she enjoyed your company. You have an open invitation to join me anytime I go." I take a pork chop bite and look into her kind eyes. "In fact, maybe you'd like to live there."

She gasps. "I don't know. I've lived here since I was a newlywed."

"It's just a thought. I realize change is hard. This morning I felt more like the sheriff than a hair stylist. It's difficult to transition sometimes."

Betty arches her eyebrows. "What made you feel like you were still in law enforcement?"

"I think one of the other students is a victim of domestic violence."

Another gulp of air from Betty. "That's terrible. Is there anything you can do?"

It's hard not to be discouraged in the system. "I hope so."

She smiles and passes me the pork chop plate. Although I'm full, I take a small piece and watch her beam. "You'll do your best, I know you will."

"Thank you. My prayer is I won't be too late."

⧗⧗⧗

Before I study my notes and required reading, I call Will to see how he and Noah are doing. I want to be intentional about trying to make a wise choice. Pastor Craig's Pilate sermon is definitely not something I want to be associated as.

"Hi, Honey. How was school? Tough to get back in the routine?" His voice is as soft as a favorite blanket.

"It was. The good news is everyone struggled, not just me. How about you and Noah?"

There's some background noise that I can't quite distinguish before Will comes back on the line. "Sorry. You asked about us?"

"Yeah. I wondered how your day was. And Noah's."

"Right. Long. A lot of deliveries. One order wasn't right."

Now I hear Noah's voice, although I can't make out what he's saying, I can tell he's talking loud. Then there's muffled sounds.

"Sorry. Noah had a question."

"Oh. Is everyone okay? Did he have a good day at school?"

"Yeah, he's fine. He wants to go to Jack Frosty's but I said no. It's a school night and he didn't finish his homework. That was one of the things you told me to do, I hope I got it right."

I hug my knees against my chest as I sit against the wall in my temporary bedroom, closing my eyes. It's an answer to prayer to have Will care so much for Noah. "You handled it perfectly. Thank you. Let me guess, Brittany was going to be there?"

He chuckles and then there's a boom that explodes through the phone.

"You aren't my dad, Will! He said I could go to Frosty's."

More muffled sounds as I'm ready to grab my purse and make a fast trek to Speculator Falls. I think I hear Will reply but Noah's impossible to ignore as he screams back.

"What do you know, anyway? My dad and mom are going to get back together. And you won't have any say over my life."

The phone went dead.

Chapter Seventeen

Hitting the call button next to Will's picture on my screen is the last thing I want to do. My hand shakes as I wait for the connection to go through. After three rings, Will answers with a brusque greeting.

"Is everything okay?" I try to sound light but I'm sure I have the same tone as a screeching owl.

"Noah's in his room for the night. We both need to cool down. Do you want to talk to him?"

I rub my temples. "In a minute. Will, about what he said."

"He just said that to get me riled, right?"

This is the perfect opportunity to confess. Own up. Spill it.

He sighs. "Carla, if there's anything I need to know, say it. If you two have feelings that need to be explored, tell me. I'd rather hurt now than be devastated by your betrayal later."

I swallow, the air in my lungs suddenly disappearing. "Will, it's…"

"It's what, Carla? I have a right to know."

Closing my eyes, the lies tumble out. "Noah's upset. He hopes Wayne and I reconnect. Right now his focus is Brittany and he's mad you won't let him go out tonight. It will all blow over tomorrow night."

I can almost feel the tension disperse over the phone. "I knew he said that to get me upset. Sorry about that." Will chuckles. "This teen stuff is new to me, but I'm in it for the long haul. Promise."

It's tempting to bang my head against the wall. Or wash my hands and pretend I can let it go like Pilate. "You're doing a great job."

Unlike me.

⧗⧗⧗

Rose perches her glasses on the tip of her nose. "I have your perm results. Some of you scored quite high." She hands a paper to Daniel and the red-colored marker with an "A" on the top bleeds through so I can see it a row away.

Sandy shuffles her position in her chair. "Wow, Daniel. You're the one to beat around here. It's almost May and you've yet to get anything below perfect."

He puts his paper face down. "Look, everyone. I've done everything but sky-write my intentions here. I have to excel. I want to open up my own place. Some of you have a lot of support back home." He looks to me. "I don't have that luxury. Few understand I want to make a difference in a way that doesn't involve medicine. People open up in their chairs. I want to encourage those clients. Help them feel beautiful inside and out."

I wait for a punchline, but his jaw is set and he's not smiling.

Sandy stretches in her seat. "We're jealous is all."

Rose hands me my paper. I receive the same grade as Daniel. Okay, I'm not envious. Today, at least.

Claire looks at her paper and says nothing. Before long she reaches into her purse and pulls out a tissue.

Mitzi tilts her head. "You okay?"

Claire shakes her head. "I'm not as good as my mom. But I want this. I need to pass."

It's Daniel who rises to the occasion. "I'll work with you."

Rose smiles. "Miss Worthington, as the semester progresses and we start working with actual clients, I do offer after hour lab times to practice with the heads. You do need to work on your book tests as well, but I believe with Mr. Garrett's help in both of those areas, you will find yourself with a cosmetology license."

Claire flashes a smile that carries some serious wattage and it looks like it's aimed right at Daniel.

"I'd be happy to help." He reached in his front pocket and pulled out his phone. "If you're free tonight, we could meet and go over notes and work in the lab. Let me make sure I have your number."

Ella, Mitzi, Sandy and I all exchange looks. Perm fumes don't seem to be the only thing in the air.

⌛⌛⌛

Although my grades are almost as good as Daniel's, I head to the library after school to study and work on Jenna's shower plans. Thanks to Shirley and Betty's help, there's little to do, but I want to make sure the decorations and favors are set. I'm tempted to work on the party first, but settle in a booth and open my notes.

A male voice greets me before I get too far into my studying. "Fancy seeing you here."

Wayne.

"Hey. What are you doing here?" I focus on keeping my voice steady.

"We had a call earlier, and Zeke left his phone here. I was closer so I said I'd look. How about you?" His eyes seemed locked on mine like lasers.

"I, uh, I'm studying. Then looking at emails for Jenna's shower."

Wayne nods. "Do you ever get out for fun? And I don't mean with your landlord for dinner." He winks.

Even though I roll my eyes, I push my book aside to make room for him to sit. For a minute. "I'm kind of busy being a mom, student, girlfriend and maid of honor."

He not only sits, he stretches in the chair and makes himself downright comfortable. "That's unacceptable. For starters, let me take you out for ice cream. Udderly Scrumptious is open."

I need somewhere else to focus on. Something safe. "No. In fact, I need to ask that you stop telling Noah we have a future together. You don't know that, and it's confusing him."

Wayne's eyebrows rise. "Okay, I won't talk about us to him. But how did Marshall take it? He couldn't love hearing that you and I have chemistry when he can barely find the friend zone."

I take in a deep breath. "Is that why you told Noah? To get at Will?"

"Not gonna lie. It was a bonus." It's tempting to slap the grin right off him.

"Listen. I admit I had trouble pushing you away once and for all. I confess I haven't been completely honest with Will. But while I've waffled around, I've paid attention. And Will is something I don't think you're interested in being."

He straightens and the smirk disappears. "What's that, Carla?"

"A mature man."

He doesn't speak for a minute or two and I'm tempted to return to my notes. Finally, he stands. "I'm the better choice for you and you know it. We're a family. Noah deserves that."

I nod. "You're right. He deserved that thirteen years ago, too."

Wayne shakes his head. "Carla, how many times do I have to apologize for something so long ago?"

"I guess when I see evidence that you're not that guy from high school who destroyed my trust in men. Because family isn't just blood or the results of a paternity test. Will has shown me and Noah that in every possible way."

This time the silence comes from Wayne stalking away. Even after he leaves, my pulse continues to race. As much as I try to concentrate on my work and Jenna's shower, I think about Will. How loving he is toward Noah and me. Affectionate. I gather my things and leave, pulling out my phone to call Will.

"Carla. I wasn't expecting to hear from you until tomorrow. Everything okay?"

His voice is like soothing cream on a blistering burn.

"Ever have a day where you just want to hear a voice that makes you feel safe?"

He chuckles. "Ever wonder why I call you so much after work?"

"No way. You always seem so collected." I unlock my car and get comfortable in my seat.

"Before I got the courage to ask you out I took my boat out a lot."

Come to think of it, he was always on the lake. "What about the winter?"

"You know the paintings on the wall in my living room?"

Ah, yes. The majestic horse. The barn scene. "I love those."

"The truth?"

I feel another knot in my stomach tighten as the most honest person I know talks about truth. "Will, what do you need to confess about those paintings?"

"Paint-by-number."

We laugh through another ten minutes of conversation. It's in those everyday chats that I feel secure in who I am and what direction I need to take. Even with Wayne's charisma, our sizzling history and the fact we have a son, Will's love for us is pure. Loyal. A Godly foundation to lay down for our family. My heart's still racing, but for different reasons.

I love Will Marshall and want to spend my life with him.

I just need the courage to tell him everything that led me to this place.

Chapter Eighteen

Gloversville's in full May bloom, as bright red and sunny yellow tulips compete with white iris for attention. There's even a burst of hues as soon as I enter the training salon. It's time to dye.

"This is what I've been waiting for." Sandy rubs her hands together as if she's a magician ready to perform.

Daniel tilts his head and furrows his brow. "Says the person with the blackest, no frills color I've ever seen."

Sandy rolls her eyes. "Dude. Do you know the people waiting for me to try colors on them? Have you seen the rainbow of colors to choose from these days? I'm stoked."

Mitzi reaches for one of the mannequin heads. "I think it will be more fun when we can color hair on clients."

Claire cinches her golden hair and wraps a band around it for a ponytail. "Not me. I'm so nervous about messing up I want to stay with the mannequins as long as possible."

Daniel moves over next to Claire's station but says nothing. Ella and I exchange looks. What's going on with Claire and Daniel, anyway?

"Maybe one of us could be a guinea pig for you before we move to the public." Daniel swivels his chair toward Claire.

Les walks in with a mannequin head and a binder. "Ready to work on color today?"

I reach for my plastic client, glad I didn't have to answer Daniel. If Claire worked on my hair before Jenna's bridal shower, I'm pretty sure my best friend would turn into Bridezilla.

Sure enough, everyone's getting their desired color results but Claire. Her platinum blonde looks more sea green. Even across the room I can see her eyes filling.

"Okay, class. That's it for today. Rose is keeping the salon open for practice until nine. Otherwise, we'll see you tomorrow." Les takes the binder and waves.

Daniel turns to Claire. "I'll stay and help."

Sandy stands and reaches for her backpack. "I wish I could. I have to work. You kids have fun."

Mitzi scoots her chair closer to Daniel and Claire. "I'm free. I'd love to help if you want it."

Claire exhales. "Thank you. I want to learn. I'm going to pass this class."

Daniel rises and strolls over to the counter, gesturing for Claire to follow him. "You'll be great. Let's find the colors for mixing. Ella? Carla? Are you two staying?"

Ella looks at her phone. "The kids are at a friend's house for a while. It would be more peaceful to get my reading done here, if that's okay."

I reach into my bag and take out my notebook. "Me, too. Claire, as much as it pains me to say it, Daniel's the best. If anyone can help you, it's him."

Everyone stops and looks my way.

"What?" I glance around and see Ella, Mitzi and Claire sporting big smiles.

Daniel has a blank stare. "Why Carla, I think that's the nicest thing you've ever said about me."

I refocus on the notes. "First time for everything."

We work until Rose strides down the spiral staircase with keys in hand. "Sorry, gang. Closing time. You'll have lots of opportunities to work on application."

Claire sighs, pushing back her plum-colored hair mannequin that was supposed to be strawberry blonde. "Ugh, there won't be enough hours in the day."

"We'll keep trying. Maybe one of us could volunteer." Daniel's voice trails off as he glances to the three of us.

Mitzi coughs and digs in her purse. "Okay, see you in the morning."

I clear my throat. "Claire, I wish I could. I'm hosting a bridal shower this weekend and then the wedding is later this month. I don't dare make any radical hair changes." I look at the doe-eyed beauty. "You know, pictures and everything."

She nods. "I understand. You guys have been great. All of you." She rests her gaze on Daniel.

"I'll do it." Ella's so bold speaking up we all do a double take.

"For real?" Claire's eyes widen.

"Are you sure?" I steal a glance at her wrist, but bracelets cover the entire area.

Ella nods. "Why not? I have a few grays coming in that could use color. I trust you."

Daniel opens the door as Rose waits behind us. "There you have it. See, Claire, nothing to worry about. Except maybe where to eat? Do you have dinner plans?"

Mitzi pipes up before Claire can. "I'm free. Do you guys want to grab some pizza?"

Ella shakes her head. "I need to get the kids. Have a good night."

"That sounds good to me. Carla?" Claire asks.

Even though I think Daniel was angling for a dinner date just with Claire, I decide to go because Mitzi is. I'm tired of studying, Betty's probably in bed, and Will told me he's working late while Noah's at Wayne's. Which gives me another night to procrastinate talking to him and confessing how close I came to losing him.

⧗⧗⧗

Ten minutes later, we're at the same restaurant where Wayne barged in and sat with Betty and me. This time, it's easy to shake his memory and focus on the company I'm with.

Mitzi flaps her menu around while talking. "Wasn't that wild when Ella volunteered to have her hair colored?"

Claire gives a slow nod. "I need the help but I don't want to mess up her life. I mean, she's a wife and mom. I don't want her to have crazy hair or anything."

Daniel bites his lip and puts his menu down. "I might be imagining things, but I have a feeling Ella's home life isn't great. She seems skittish."

Claire sets her menu to the side. "You're right. Remember that snowstorm when her husband came in? He didn't seem very nice."

Daniel turns to me. "So, former sheriff, what do you think?"

I look around the table. All eyes are on me. "I think we have a right to be concerned. She's an adult, though, and she volunteered to have her hair colored. The rest," I visualize the bruises. "I think we need to pay attention. If we see anything unusual, let's speak up."

The three promise as the waitress saunters over and takes our orders.

Once she leaves, Mitzi rests her arms on the table and leans in. "So, Carla, tell us your fierce stories as sheriff. You could totally have your own reality show or something. From sheriff to stylist. It's fascinating." Her hair bobs in rhythm to her fast chatter.

Daniel chuckles. "I have to admit, I'm curious too. I can't picture a petite thing like you taking down a perp."

Claire laughs and Daniel smiles back at her.

Mitzi and I exchange winks, and the other two have no idea.

"Thankfully we have a very safe county. I dealt with drugs, domestic violence, speeding, and the out-of-state hunter that killed a pet and not a deer."

Mitzi's eyes grow wide. "For real?"

I nod. "I also had to distract a bear for traffic to pass on Rte. 30."

Claire slaps her manicured hand on the table. "You have the best life, Carla."

At first I open my mouth to protest, but I stop. There's Noah, Will. The amazing gift where I'm able to go to school and start a salon. I have wonderful friends here and in Speculator Falls. No more beating myself up. No more Pilate deals, as Pastor would say. "Thanks, Claire. I feel really blessed."

Mitzi leans back in her chair as the waitress brings our appetizers. "Speaking of Will, you two going to get married? Or is he nervous about Noah's father?"

Okay, I *was* feeling blessed.

Chapter Nineteen

It's a hasty exit out of school Thursday evening so I can pick up Betty and head back to Speculator Falls for Jenna's shower.

"I'll take notes for you tomorrow." Daniel promises as I find my keys.

"I'm going to put Claire's hair color practice on Ella on YouTube." Sandy winks at me as she teases. At least I think she's teasing.

"Thanks, everyone. Try not to have too much fun without me." I lift my Yankees lanyard and jog to the door. The group waves and I realize with the extra day off to prepare for Jenna's party, I'm going to miss my GBS colleagues.

An hour later Betty and I are heading north for home, my mind reeling with to-do tasks for the shower and the big goal for the weekend: talk to Will. I'm not sure if my hand is shaking from nerves or two energy drinks.

"Make sure you let me help, Carla. I know Shirley and the senior center volunteers have done a lot, but I can be an extra set of hands." Betty's calm voice stops my mental checklist.

I glance at her. "You're a blessing. I hope you know that. The seniors are very proud of Jenna, and if I mess this up, I'll never hear the end of it."

She chuckles. "I can't imagine them doing anything but loving you. After all, Will delivers meals to them each day. They are all fond of you both from what Sara told me."

Until they hear I nearly decided Wayne was a better choice for a boyfriend.

A light rain prompts me to turn on the wipers. "I appreciate that. And, after this weekend, I hope they're right."

⧗⧗⧗

Once we pull in the driveway, Will sprints off the sidewalk and is at my side of the car to greet me. The light mist is now a steady downfall but he seems ambivalent as he opens the door and takes my hand.

"I've been like a kid waiting for the okay to come downstairs Christmas morning. I'm so glad you're here for a long weekend." He focuses on Betty. "Welcome back, Betty. We're all happy you came for another visit."

She waves him off. "You're too sweet. Now kiss that girl of yours. I can get out of the truck just fine. Is Noah here?"

In my addled state I try to remember his schedule.

Will shakes his head. "He's at work."

Betty nods. "Ah. I baked some cookies for him. Oh, well. I'll head in and put them in the kitchen. You two take your time." She winks.

When Will lowers his head toward mine, my heartbeat accelerates. It's not fear or waffling, its anticipation. This man loves me, flaws and all. And I can't wait to feel his gentle touch.

His kiss is tender but takes my breath when it lasts longer than I'm used to for a greeting. When he breaks off the embrace, he's wearing a grin. "I've been waiting all week for this moment."

I reach for his collar and hold it for a moment. "You make me wish I didn't have most of this weekend tied up with the shower."

"We'll have time together, I'll make sure of it." He cups his hands around my face and kisses me again before stepping back. "But first, there's a dinner at Jack Frosty's. Sara invited us and insists on paying. Betty, too. Ben and Jenna will be there once he closes the store."

I open my mouth to ask about Noah, but Will keeps talking.

"Noah's going out to Josh's house to play video games. We'll pick him up after dinner."

"You know me too well."

He reaches for my hand and gives it a squeeze. "Not as much as I'd like to. We need to steal away this weekend and talk. I feel like God is saying so much about us."

My lips still tingle from his touch. "I'd like that. I wanted to do the same."

Will lets go of my hand and walks to the back of the truck to retrieve our bags. "Babe, I think this is going to be a life changing weekend."

I close my eyes and take a breath. *Please, Lord, let me be honest with Will and help him understand. Now that I know what I have, I don't want to lose him.*

⧗⧗⧗

The sun tucks under the mountains and the stars are out as Sara, Betty, Jenna, Ben, Will and I finish the last of our dinners. With Will's arm draped around my shoulder, I watch Ben with Jenna. He can't keep his eyes off her. The serious businessman looks positively goofy.

Betty takes a sip of water. "Are you ready for your shower, Jenna?"

She sits straighter in the booth, her face glowing. "I'm so excited. It's all the seniors have been talking about. Shirley probably is re-working her clipboard as we speak. But the day I really can't wait for is the wedding day." Jenna glances toward Ben.

"I'm with you. I keep looking at the app on my phone that tracks the time left until you are Mrs. Jenna Regan. At first I was annoyed Noah and his friends put that thing on there, but now I stare at it all the time."

Sara looks to her grandson. "You remind me so much of your grandfather. You two have such a bright future ahead of you. Jenna, how are your parents doing? Are they okay that the wedding is here and not in Ohio?"

Jenna wipes her mouth with her napkin and then places it on her finished plate. "They were surprised at first but now they're excited. They plan to bring a lot of Youngstown wedding traditions here. I'm excited to share it all with you."

I could tear up watching the excitement bubble out of her. "First, we need to have your shower."

Jenna looks at her watch and sighs. "True. I suppose I better head home. It's a long day tomorrow." She reaches for her purse. "But I know it will be an amazing one. Thanks, Carla. You're the best."

Will playfully elbows my arm. "Yeah, Carla. You are." He then focuses on Sara. "Sara, do you mind taking Betty back to Carla's? We have some things we want to talk about."

Jenna giggles and whispers as she passes by me to get her umbrella. "Double wedding."

Sara replies to Will so I can ignore Jenna. "Absolutely. Take your time. I'll keep Betty company."

Betty smiles. "I'd enjoy that. Take your time, kids."

Once Wendy the manager picks up the last of our plates, Sara insists on paying for our meals. Ben announces he'll take care of the tip. We gather our things and most everyone heads to the front. I linger for a moment as Ben digs in his pocket.

"Ben, I wanted to say something. We go way back, and you're marrying my best friend."

He looks up, brows arched, as he pulls out a stack of bills. "This about Will? Or Wayne?"

I bite my lip. "Yes. You deserve to know Wayne did pursue me. And I was tempted. Briefly. I'm going to confess that to Will tonight. And tell him how deeply committed I am to him."

The money drops on the table. "You mean it? You aren't responding to pressure? Because Wayne will always be in the picture."

"I understand. Will is the one I love. But any future we have needs to be founded on Christ and based on trust. I wanted you to know."

Ben clears his throat. "Will is the most decent guy Speculator Falls could ever know, next to my grandpa."

My voice catches. "I know."

Suddenly, he smiles. "And you, Carla Rowling, are one of the strongest women in all the Adirondack Mountains. You're the perfect fit for Will."

⌛⌛⌛

Twenty minutes later Will and I stroll down the sidewalk to Moffitt Beach. There's a park bench next to the lamp post. If that's not enough accountability, Pastor and Brooke live across the street.

"So, finally alone." Will sighs.

"Seems impossible these days, doesn't it?" I sit facing him.

"It's short term. At least, that's what I wanted to talk about."

I suck in a gasp of air. This conversation isn't going where I think it is, is it?

"Okay. Well, may I speak first? It's important." Are my words stuttering? Ears ringing?

He places his hand on top of mine. "Absolutely."

Here goes nothing.

"There've been so many changes this year. Howard's gift, Noah transitioning into a teenager, leaving the sheriff's department, starting school, Jenna's wedding, Wayne being back. It's been a lot more stressful than I've let on."

Will caresses my shaking hand. "You've handled it like a champ. Seriously, Carla. I don't know how you balance it all, but you do."

A nervous laugh escapes. "Not as well as you think. I need to tell you something. I should have earlier."

I can't tell with the lamppost glare if he's starting to pale. But he takes away his hand and wipes it on his jeans.

"This sounds heavy."

"That fight you and Noah had the night I was on the phone. He mentioned Wayne, and I laughed it off."

His head bobs as he kicks at some rocks. "I remember."

I take a breath in hopes of steadying myself but a messy sob rushes out. "Wayne told me he had feelings. He asked me to make a choice."

Will jumps up and starts pacing in front of the bench. "What? How long ago?"

"I don't know the exact date. But what I wanted you to know is…"

He doesn't wait. "You chose him. Of course you did. He's the father of your child."

I stand and try to reach out to him, but he's weaving like a boxer. "That isn't it at all. I choose you. But I wanted to be honest and let you know there was a season Wayne wanted me to consider leaving you. I didn't, and I told him so."

He stops and there's complete silence for what feels like a full minute. A sound comes out but I can't tell if it's a laugh or a grunt. Or something altogether different. "Let me get this straight. A while ago, as in longer than days or weeks ago, probably months, Wayne confessed his feelings for you. Wayne who ran the second you told him you were pregnant. The guy Noah rarely saw until he moved here almost a year ago. He asked you to make a choice between him and me."

I nod, even though he isn't looking at me.

"And then, you don't tell me. Even when I straight up ask."

"Will, I'm sorry. I handled it poorly." I sound like a small child on her way to the timeout chair.

"So you held information from me and you lied. Am I following this correctly?" His voice rises to a level I've never heard from him before.

Desperation taints my plea. "Please forgive me. That sermon at Easter really helped me understand I had to make a choice, that I was being unfair to you."

He sits down on the bench and buries his face in his hands.

I brush a tear from the corner of my eye. "Will? Say something. Please."

Will shakes his head. "You never said a word. Then you lied. That's not even the worst of it." He stands and gestures for me to follow. He's on a fast track back to where his car is. "You took months to decide."

I sprint to catch up. "I know. So foolish of me."

"Carla, I get I'm not a handsome, charismatic guy like Wayne. I hear the flannel jokes. But there's no one that loves more deeply than I do. I took care of Noah without hesitation. I did everything you ever asked and plenty more you never did. And you had to think about who to choose. For months."

Our voices seem to break together, but it's the only unity we have between us. Since Noah's accident at school, I've never felt more fear. Not even when Wayne left. "Can you forgive me?"

He unlocks his truck and opens the door for me, something that only triggers more of my tears. "I need some space Carla."

Okay. At least he's speaking to me.

"Right. Did you want to meet up after the shower?"

He starts the vehicle. "I don't think so."

I nearly double over from the pain I feel. "You wanted to talk. Is it too late?"

It's another long pause before I barely hear his reply. "Please give me some space. It's the very least you could do."

Chapter Twenty

Even hidden in the bathroom lifting the wet washcloth off my eyes, I still look red and puffy. Every time I think about Will's parting words and remember the silence as he dropped me off, I recite that this is Jenna's day. There's no way I want her to know. In fact, my coward heart doesn't want anyone to realize Will reacted just as I deserve.

There's a knock on the door followed by a teen's deepening yet squeaky voice. "Mom, Ben's picking me up in a few minutes for work, then after we'll go to the shower to help pack up the stuff. Is Will meeting us there?"

Another look in the mirror. There's no way I can pull this off. I open the door and paste on a smile. "No, sweetie. I think it's you two. I'll help, though."

He nods, his bangs falling into his eyes. I need to cut those.

"Oh. Is he working?"

No more lies. But he can't know. Not yet. "No, he just said he can't be there."

That seems to satisfy him as he saunters down the hall.

I walk to my room and look inside my closet. The party dresses all look so bright and festive. Today's the day I want to dress and appear as drab as Daniel always accuses me of possessing. I pull out a tan pair of capris and a purple short-sleeved blouse.

As soon as I arrive in the kitchen I find Betty at the table with a full cup of coffee in front of her. "Busy day today. You should get some caffeine in you."

I sit and try not to look at her. "Thanks. I definitely need energy."

"You want to talk about it?"

Okay, now I have to face her. "I'm sorry?"

She reaches over and pats my arm. "Carla, Will dropped you off last night without walking you to the door and roared off like he was losing a drag race. You waved goodnight to Sara and me and went straight to your room. And, I think I heard you crying throughout the night." Her blue eyes are so kind and safe.

A shudder accents the cry I can't contain. "I took Will for granted. Last night I confessed some things, and he asked for space. I lost him, Betty."

She stands and immediately walks over with arms outstretched. "Oh, honey. I'm sorry."

I rise, body shaking from sobs. "The look he had when I told the truth. I'll never forget it."

Betty strokes my hair as she holds me. "Things will seem better. They always do. Give him some time."

"I'm not sure. Everything seemed so final."

She steps back and waves her hand. "My husband and I had quite the spat when we were engaged. I had cold feet and didn't dare let on. He knew, but he wanted me to trust him enough to tell him. I didn't. And when it all came out, he was furious. It took two weeks, two long, miserable weeks, but we both came around."

"What if he won't look after Noah while I'm at school? What if he won't talk to him, either? It will crush Noah."

Betty chuckled. "I can't picture Will doing such a thing." She walks to her suitcase. "Now, we have a shower to attend. Let's focus on that, and we'll face everything else later."

I nod and take a sip of coffee. "Thanks, Betty. You're a godsend."

She digs into her luggage and pulls out an envelope. "You're sweet. It's you who has been an answer to prayer for me. Okay. I have a card and money ready for Jenna. Let me know when you're ready."

With another swig of black liquid, I walk over to my purse and open up my compact. Still puffy, but thankfully, all eyes will be on Jenna.

⧗⧗⧗

Two hours later, Jenna walks through the threshold in a robin's egg, lace dress with her hair still intact in the bun we created an hour before. Not even all the candlelight can compete with the glow she carries as she greets everyone.

Shirley escorts her to the head table. All the guests stand and clap as Jenna takes a seat.

"You guys are too much," Jenna gushes. "But I love it."

Laughter fills the air. Shirley grabs a microphone off the table and turns it on. "We love you, Jenna, and hope this shower blesses you. It's a busy afternoon so let's get started." She consults her clipboard. "First, let's fill the other seats at the head table."

I'm not sure what Shirley's up to. There are three seats up front, but I'm the only local bridesmaid. My head's too foggy to remember what we wrote on the agenda.

"Okay. I'm ready for anything." Jenna couldn't stop smiling even if someone wired her jaw shut. It was months ago she overreacted with Ben and was certain they were done.

God, please let Will and I have a happy ending.

Shirley grips the microphone and turns so the audience and the guest of honor can see her. "Good thing because I have a surprise for you. Jenna, your mom and sister, Megan, are here!"

Two women emerge from behind the threshold and run to the front. Jenna jumps up and squeals, throwing her arms around the two in a group hug that's instantly surrounded by happy tears.

That Shirley is a genius. I didn't even think of having her family travel from Ohio for this. Another regret seizes my stomach.

The trio breaks apart and faces the crowd. Black streaks line Jenna's cheeks but it doesn't take away from her beauty.

Jenna looks toward Shirley's direction, then mine. "You guys, how did you pull this off?" She turns to her mom and younger sister. "And you two. No one said a word. I can't believe it, especially after I called whining about how far away you were from here."

Meg looks like Jenna's clone except for lighter, shoulder length hair. "It wasn't easy. So, where are all the single lumberjacks?"

More laughter. My queasy stomach tightens again. What I'd give to see Will walk through in his plaid flannel shirt.

Servers appear with carts full of food. It feels like the room is closing in as voices mingle and I keep seeing Will walk away. Suddenly Shirley's edict booms through the microphone.

"Carla. When we decided to have you pray over the meal I didn't mean in silence. C'mon up and get the microphone."

I attempt to giggle but it isn't there as I march toward Jenna's right hand woman at the senior center. "Sorry, I kind of spaced for a moment."

"Well, get with it girl. You're up after lunch with games."

Yeah, games. The thing I've been playing for months and no longer want to be around.

⧖⧖⧖

Three hours, four games and probably two hundred sheets of tissue paper and gift bags later, Ben and Noah dismantle the balloon threshold and start taking presents to Ben's truck. Most of the guests are gone and Shirley sits with her shoes off, rubbing her foot.

I sit across from her. "You did an amazing job. I never thought about Jenna's family."

"You live as long as me, you'll have been to your share of parties. I thought it would be a great surprise for everyone." Her large brown eyes look tired.

"It was. You sit and rest. I'll handle clean up." I pat her arm as I stand and walk to the table next to her.

"You're a good girl, Carla. Thanks."

I stack the dirty dishes and head to the kitchen when Ben looks up, says something to Noah, and walks toward me.

"Hey." He starts picking up utensils at the same table.

"Hi, Ben. You have quite the haul to take back to the house." I don't look up, but keep stacking dishes.

"Will stopped by today." I nearly drop the saucer I picked up. "So you know?"

He reaches for the empty water pitcher. "That Will's hurting? Yes."

Tears threaten and I turn to another table, but Ben apparently knows avoidance when he sees it.

He closes in on the distance between us and puts the jug down. "He'll come around, Carla."

I nod, still not able to look him in the eyes. "I should have told the truth from the beginning. I was a fool."

148

He chuckled. "Some of us learn the hard way. You do remember how I treated Jenna when she first moved here, right?"

Oh, right. There wasn't a more wounded man with a wall of defense to surround him from being hurt again.

"Okay, so we aren't perfect. What do you suggest?"

Ben reaches for the water once again. "What did Will say?"

My breathing comes out as small jags of emotion. "To give him space."

"Men need time to process. Let him pray and figure things out. I've never seen Will hold a grudge. I'm sure you'll see him ready to talk sooner than later." Ben sounds so confident, I can't help but stand taller and find new energy as I stack more saucers.

But fear still lurks. "What if it takes him later?"

Ben starts to walk to the kitchen, but turns. "Then you can talk to him at church. I told him he better be there."

Chapter Twenty-One

I could return to Gloversville early and avoid church. As soon as I wake, the excuses run through my mind faster than I ever have on a track. I don't want to see Will, not during service when I'm not sure how he's feeling toward me. But I'm also done dodging reality. If I leave, I miss time with Noah. And I still have to tell him that Will's upset.

Running sounds easier.

Once I shower and dress, it's time to chat with Noah. We don't have a lot of time before church, and I pray the conversation doesn't take a lot of directions I'm not ready for.

"Hey, Noah? Got a minute?" I knock three times on his bedroom door.

He opens it before I can wait for a reply. "What's up?"

I make tentative steps to his bed, covered in clothes that I can't discern are clean or dirty. He's opening dresser drawers and then pulls out a pair of socks.

"There's no easy way to say this but you deserve to know." I glance over at the teen who seems more focused on putting on his socks. "Will and I are taking a little break."

Noah drops the sock and raises his head. "You broke up?"

Yes. No. I don't know.

"I believe Will needs some time to sort things out. But in no way does this affect you."

He bends down and grabs the white footwear. "You sure? It's going to be awkward."

"Will isn't like that at all. I thought I should tell you since I don't plan to sit with him. It's important to me to honor his wishes."

"Whatever. Just tell me when things change. Can I ask a question?"

"Always."

"Does this have anything to do with me? Or Dad?"

The gasp I hear is my own. "Absolutely not you. It's about me not being as communicative and open as I could have been."

He nods. "About Dad?"

"Okay. I'll share a bit here, but make sure you're ready for church. Betty's probably heading to the car, waiting for us."

Noah finishes putting on the socks and walks to the closet where he pulls out a pair of shoes. "Dad feels bad about abandoning you."

I stand and work on navigating a clear path to the door. "He rejected both of us for a long time. But, he's changed a lot. For the better. Still, I don't see a future with him. Not a romantic one. And I wish I'd been more open about that fact with both of them."

Noah's right behind me. "Will's good for you, Mom. I understand what you're saying about Dad. I'm glad he's in my life and all, but there's something special about you and Will."

This kid never ceases to amaze me. We walk together down the hall and find Betty in the kitchen, Bible in hand.

I put my arm around my son. "Thanks, Noah. Let's pray Will and I can overcome this."

Betty smiles as she heads for the door. "If anyone can beat the obstacles, it's you."

⏳⏳⏳

Before the small choir can sing a note, I march down the center aisle and make a beeline for the pew where Sara, Ben and Jenna sit. They move down and as the music track starts, Betty and I take our seats. Even when I glance around to see if Noah's sitting with Brittany, there's no sight of Will.

Jenna leans over and whispers into my ear. "We need to talk, girl."

I clear my throat and open my bulletin, hoping she takes the hint that now isn't a good time.

Ben places his hand in hers. "It can wait."

Phew.

My eyes zoom in on the altar area and stay there through worship, announcements, and when Pastor Craig approaches the podium. If Will's behind me in another pew, I'm unaware, but my hands shake just the same as I dig for a pencil to take notes.

"Today we're talking about Lazarus and his resurrection." Pastor

Craig grips the lectern and smiles. "There are a lot of sermons to share when it comes to him. Take the grave clothes off, for one. Come forth is another. My focus is on Mary."

Ah, Mary. The sister that sits at His feet. Anoints the Lord. Let's see where this goes.

"We are in John, chapter eleven. Lazarus, definitely someone important to Jesus as he was referred to as 'he whom You love,' has taken sick and it's serious enough that Mary and Martha send word to Jesus. Now, if Brooke and I were away for some reason and we received word that any of you were ill, I'd be back here without hesitation."

I glance to Brooke, who nods.

"But not Jesus. He waits. When He finally journeys to Bethany, they're informed Lazarus has been buried for four days. Forget sick or even recently deceased. He's been prepared with oils, wrapped and entombed. Imagine the grief Mary and Martha must be feeling."

What if this was Noah? Or Will? Goosebumps dot my arms.

"And Jesus shows up and wants to talk. Mary, the one who displayed such love for her Lord and He decides not to help save her brother. And He wants to talk to her? I've tried to place myself there and the emotions are so deep and charged, I can't even begin to accurately picture it. But, there's a song I remember hearing a few years back that tells the story so well."

Jenna looks to me and shrugs.

"It's a Southern Gospel song about Martha meeting up with Jesus. The questions, accusation, even. 'Lord, if You had been here, my brother would be here, was the gist of it." Jesus? He's not offended. In fact, I believe He's overcome with compassion and love. This family means a lot to Him. So, He asks to see the grave."

As Pastor sets up the scene, I try to picture myself there. Mary's reaction is exactly how I'd feel. Her question is one I ask a lot under less adversity, *Lord, where are You?*

"You know the miracle. Jesus, in His authority, proclaims that Lazarus come forth. And he does. Rotten linens attached to him, but he's alive. Do you think anyone in that crowd cares how Lazarus looks or smells? Jesus brought the guy back from the dead. Where do you think Mary's faith level is?"

Um, probably sky high.

"And where would it have been had Jesus shown up when Lazarus was only sick?" He walks away from the podium. "That's the rub. At least for me it is. I want things easy. Who wants pain or suffering? No one I know. But sometimes Jesus allows a wait in our lives to teach us something we'd never learn without the hurt."

Okay, I can relate to this. And I don't like it.

"The song talked about Jesus being late. That's how Martha saw it when Jesus finally reached her. But in His divine way, He wasn't tardy. Can you come to the same conclusion with your situation? Are you waiting on a job interview or a doctor report? Friends, Christ is not late. He is right on time. Do you believe that?"

If Pastor Craig's sermon were a symphony, his last line would have been a crescendo. "If you can relate, there's grace available. Feel free to meet God right where you are, or come to the altar. Whatever you do, don't leave feeling bitter because you think He didn't show up on time."

Even sitting up front, it takes time to reach the altar. A crowd gathers as Jay Maxwell plays the guitar quietly on stage.

Brooke is once again at my side without questions or judgement. "Father, help Carla put and keep her trust in You. Give her the strength to see things in Your way. Help her understand You aren't late in meeting the desires of her heart. Thank You for being on time."

Tears fall to the carpet because Brooke says exactly what I fear. I'll stop trusting Him. Again. I'll do it my way and mess everything up as I usually do. That I want to be patient in waiting for Will to come around, but I'm afraid he won't.

She opens her eyes and gives me a hug, something I look forward to each week. "God knows your heart, Carla. How I wish you knew how much He loves you."

I nod, unable to speak. The magnitude of His love and plan are too much.

Brooke squeezes my arm and moves to the next person. I close my eyes and continue to pray. When I finish, I attempt to quietly make it back to my seat, but I bump into someone deep in prayer with Pastor Craig.

Will.

☒☒☒

Jenna ambushes me in the lobby after I quietly skirt past Will, and before I can find Betty and Noah to make a fast exit. "Why didn't you tell me about Will?"

"It was your bridal shower. Your day. I wasn't going to ruin your special day."

She shakes her head. "You wouldn't have. How can I help?"

Out of the corner of my eye I spot Will leaving the sanctuary and heading our way.

I bite my lip for a moment, then lean closer to my best friend. "Pray for me."

Jenna gives me a quick hug as Will approaches. God bless her, she stays.

"Will, hi." My smile feels as flat as my hair.

He also manages a grin, albeit not a very wide one. "Hey, Jenna. Carla." No hug. No handshake. Nothing. "Good service, right?"

Jenna nods. "Pastor Craig always has wisdom for us." She glances at me. "So, I'm sure you two need to talk without me in the middle. Carla, call me. Will, see you around." She's gone before I can beg her to stay.

My heartbeat threatens to implode as my body seems to shut down one system at a time. With a dry throat, I attempt to speak. "I'm so sorry."

He holds up his hand. "I know, but I'm still not ready. I'm stuck on the fact it took you so long to choose, and then you lied. It hurts, Carla." His voice squeaks when he says my name.

Even swallowing doesn't help. It's like someone massaged my tonsils with sandpaper.

"But I won't leave you in a lurch with Noah. I'll still help out. That's all I wanted to say." He turns and makes his way to the exit, the faint trail of his cologne lasting longer than our conversation.

Chapter Twenty-Two

The smell of bacon is the only reason I'm semi-quick rising out of bed when the alarm rings. It's the first day back to school, and my heart feels like an anchor dragging everything else in my life down.

"Good morning, Carla. I thought you'd need some extra fuel with your schedule today. I know it's a long day for you after a pretty intense weekend. I have bacon, toast, and blueberry pancakes." Betty even wears a faded floral apron as she does her work. My childhood dream came true to have someone make a breakfast overflowing with love.

"This is amazing." I walk over and give her a hug. "Betty, you're outstanding."

She rolls her eyes and spreads a slab of butter on a piece of toast.

"Can I ask you something?" I reach for a few slices of bacon to add to my pancake plate.

"Of course, dear. What's on your mind?"

"What will you do when I graduate?" The maple syrup spreads all over my pancakes.

Betty stops for a moment as if she were pondering my question. "Honestly, I haven't given it a lot of thought. I've had boarders before, but none that I've grown as close to as you. It won't be the same without you around."

I savor the bacon before cutting a piece of the moist pancake with my fork. "Whatever you do, I hope you won't be a stranger."

⧖⧖⧖

Brandi smiles, glances down at the desk and quickly looks back my way once I walk past her.

"Good morning?" The phone rings, but she holds up a manicured finger before I can sprint away. Once Brandi completes the call she tilts her head as if she were inspecting me. "You okay, Carla?"

Probably those puffy eyes of mine.

"It was a long weekend. I'm ready to focus on classes and application."

She takes a sip of her drink and raises that same finger. "Wait! That reminds me, I'm supposed to give you this hand-out."

I step back to the desk and take the paper. "What's this?"

"Hours that the salon is open to the public and the way you get your clinical hours in. Starts for you in June."

The paper suddenly feels like a brick. It's one thing to work on the mannequin heads. But to finally give perms, tapered cuts and complicated colors to real people makes this feel a lot more real than I'm ready for.

With paper in hand, I make my way upstairs to the classroom.

Daniel's already there stirring his coffee when he spots me. "Do you know how bad your eyes look?"

I dump my backpack, purse and the paper on my desk. "How many times do I have to tell you that even with perfect hair skills, you won't have any clients with a personality like yours?"

He raises his hands in surrender. "Okay, I'm sorry. It's just, wow. You look like you have a horrible hangover or something."

"Not quite. I really don't want to talk much about it. I'll leave it at Will doesn't want to see me right now." Just saying his name hurts my heart.

Daniel sits next to me. "Hey, Carla. I'm sorry. I hope it works out. Really."

If I think too hard about it, tears will take over. I manage a small smile. "See? Now that's the kind of compassion that will give you a great reputation."

Sandy, Mitzi, Ella and Claire follow Rose into the room. Before Daniel can reply, Rose introduces the new unit.

"It's usually at this point students feel overwhelmed, wondering 'when does all this end?' Les and I schedule this unit here as a bit of a break. The lessons are still important and something you'll use often, but a switch from constant hair techniques. Any guesses?" Rose slides her glasses down her nose and scans the crowd.

Mitzi raises her hand. "Business items?"

Rose shakes her head. "No, we save that for last."

Sandy plays with her pencil as she smirks. "Weaves?"

I try to picture the bulk of our year 'round Speculator Falls residents, many senior citizens, who would request hair extensions or weaves.

"No, but artificial hair is coming up soon. Anyone else?"

Claire looks around and then raises her hand. "Facials?"

Rose nods. "That's right. Let's talk about facials and then learn how to create and apply ones that will have your clients raving."

⧖⧖⧖

Before we break for lunch, Rose invites us to try different facials. Some are from high-end salons, some from department stores, and she even said a few were mixes she'd found on Pinterest. When we decide to eat together at the hot dog shop, my skin feels like a smooth, cool winter's afternoon thanks to the Pinterest mix I rinsed off.

Daniel opens the door for us. "Claire, what kind did you use?"

She swings her purse as she walks past him. "I, um, kind of made my own concoction. Rose said it was okay. She's going to try it while we're gone. It's something I play around with at home."

Sandy looks to me and shrugs.

Mitzi picks up her pace to catch up with Claire. "You know, maybe this is an answer for you."

Daniel also jogs so he can join us as we walk the two blocks to the shop.

Claire slows down. "What do you mean?"

"A lot of salons offer more than one service. Maybe there would be one that would want someone to provide facials and makeup. Perhaps that's what you're meant to do."

Daniel nods. "That's true, especially if you're in a bigger city."

Claire sighs. "Let's see what Rose says. She might hate what I've done." Another sigh. "Like everything else I've tried so far. But, if she loves it, it's something to consider."

Daniel clears his throat. "Lake George is a perfect place for your talents."

Ella smiles and nudges me. "Daniel, isn't that where you're based?"

Mitzi, Sandy and I share a giggle as we walk inside. Although neither Claire nor Daniel answer Ella, she does sit next to him.

"So, Ella. When are you letting Claire color your hair?" Sandy asks as she inspects her silverware.

"Tonight. My husband is working late and the kids are with friends. I'm excited."

Claire coughs. "Thanks again, Ella, for volunteering." She turns to Daniel. "And to you for offering to help me."

Daniel nods. "No problem. You're going to get the hang of everything." He winks in Claire's direction. "I promise."

It's a look I recognize and my throat feels like it's closing in. Last year Will winked and nudged me during Ben's barbeque. It was the start of looking at him as more than a friend.

"Carla. You okay?"

I blink several times and realize Ella's waving her hand in front of me. "Sorry. I was thinking about something."

Mitzi leans in. "Anything you want to talk about?"

I purse my lips as I think about how much I want to share when the waitress appears. Once she takes our orders and leaves, I sigh. "My mind's on overload. Will and I had a rough weekend and things are up in the air."

Even Mitzi, the constant smile amongst us, frowns when I explain.

"Dude, that's terrible." Sandy finally puts the fork down on the napkin.

Ella's voice is softer than usual. "I hope you two can work it out. A good relationship is hard to find."

I nod and glance at Daniel. Is he wondering if she's talking about her own life? Because I am.

"Thanks, everyone. He's asked for some time. I messed things up. He's hurting." Each word becomes harder to speak as my throat continues to constrict.

Sandy leans back as the waitress arrives with our meals. "Don't give him too much time."

"What's too much?" Mitzi reaches for a French fry.

"I don't know but out of sight, out of mind."

Daniel rolls his eyes. "You don't believe that, do you?"

Sandy looks around the restaurant. "Do you see me with anyone?"

He shakes his head.

Sandy allows a small smile to escape. "That's what I'm saying, Carla. You should text him. He might not be ready to chat, but at least he'll know you care. Trust me."

I lift my hot dog and take a bite. "You might have a point."

She narrows her eyebrows. "I know I do."

⧖⧖⧖

When school dismisses for the day I watch Ella, Claire and Daniel move from the classroom to the salon area.

Mitzi waves as she walks to the exit. "Can't wait to see the results."

Sandy holds up her phone. "Text us updates." She turns to me. "Contact the guy."

I blow enough hot air out to move my bangs. "I will when I get in my truck." I turn to the trio. "I'll be praying."

"We won't need it." Daniel sounds confident, but Claire's shaky wave goodbye doesn't look as strong.

Once I'm in the truck, I slide my phone out of my purse and slide to my message screen. I start typing his contact info and his picture pops up. How I miss that kind smile.

Just checking in to once again ask your forgiveness. And to let you know I love you.

As I reach Betty's, eat dinner, study and put my pajamas on, I reach for my phone every few minutes. There's texts from Noah. Pictures from Claire revealing Ella's gorgeous black color with mahogany and copper ombre highlights.

I type a quick encouragement. *Claire! Amazing job. WTG!*

Within thirty seconds, a reply. *Thx. Daniel helped so much. Ella's beaming.*

She should! So what's up with you and Daniel?

161

Before Claire responds, my text notification rings.
Will.

.

Chapter Twenty-Three

My insides still feel hollow the next morning as I stare at Will's words on my phone screen.

Thx. Still not ready to talk.

Perhaps it's time to consider life without Will. I don't want to. I hate the thought for Noah. It's not fair to force his hand and beg him back into our lives. Before I leave for class, I sit on my bed and re-read my notes from Pastor Craig's sermon on waiting. *No matter what happens, it's important to believe God's right on time.*

My heart's heavy as I enter the classroom. I push away thoughts of Will and notice Daniel and Claire sitting together. Smiling. Laughing.

I take a seat ahead of them and turn around. "It's the dynamic hair coloring duo."

Claire rests her hand on his arm. "Daniel was amazing. Not only did he help me with the color, but I never would have thought I could have done the highlights. Ella left looking like a model."

Daniel nods. "She really does. I can't wait for you to see her."

Sandy folds her arms. "Where is she?"

He shrugs. "You know Ella, she's usually the last one here."

Claire brushes a piece of her hair away from her eye. "You guys are going to freak when you see her. The color is even bolder in person. The way the black slowly transforms to red by the ends, it's amazing."

Sandy nods, but there's no smile from that tough critic. "It sounds epic. Let's hope she gets here before Les does."

When our teacher arrives and closes the door, we glance at each other. Ella's not here.

By lunch dismissal, Daniel's the first to meet me at my desk. "Carla, she wasn't sick. Her kids were okay. I have a bad feeling that something happened to Ella."

Claire, Mitzi and Sandy join him as I stand and reach for my purse.

"Did anyone try to contact her?"

Mitzi nods. "I texted her right before class started. No answer."

I tap my nails on the desk as I think. "We can't jump to conclusions. I have a lot of experience with everything being fine at home one minute, and then ten minutes later I was turning around because of Noah suddenly being sick. Maybe she had car trouble."

Mitzi narrows her eyes. "Or her husband didn't appreciate her transformation."

The others nod. The sick feeling in my gut agrees, but this could get out of control. Fast.

"Try calling her. There's not a lot we can do right now."

Claire's bottom lip quivers. "What if she's in trouble?"

Daniel sighs. "We pray she's protected."

"He's right. Who knows? Maybe before the next class Ella will come walking in, laughing at how something silly made her late. I've seen it a lot in my old sheriff days. Family members jumped to conclusions, called us in, and the person was fine." But not always.

Sandy nudges me with her elbow. "I vote you pray for her."

I look around and see wide eyes, solemn faces and nodding heads. I'm the oldest in the group, and the only other mom. "Okay. I'm learning that no matter how messy life gets, prayer is key." Will's text comes to mind, but I refuse to forget Mary, Martha and Lazarus and how Christ shows up every time. "Heavenly Father, we ask that You place Ella in Your hands and protect her. If she's in trouble, connect her with the right people who can help. If she's having an off day, give her the strength as a wife and mom to see her situation through. Thank You that we have Your Son to turn to, good days and bad. It is in His name we give thanks. Amen and Amen."

A chorus of "Amens" erupt, and it hits me. These people are like a second family.

⌛⌛⌛

No one is in the mood for lunch so we stay in the room until Rose enters for our afternoon session on makeup. Even across the room I can see the sparkle in Claire's eyes as we hear about foundation, blush, and eyeshadows.

Rose stops in front of Daniel. "Salons are more versatile these days. It's no longer a place full of perms and haircuts. If you have a goal of opening your own place, consider offering manicures. Facials. Makeup application. Waxing. Weddings and proms alone should make these opportunities profitable in no time."

I never thought of that. All I keep seeing is a little house in Speculator Falls with the sign Will and Noah made swinging in the breeze. Daniel? His expression looks like he found the blueprints to a treasure as Rose keeps talking.

Class has about another thirty minutes when my phone vibrates. Could this be Will? I flip it over to peek at the screen.

Wayne.

I slide the screen and look at the message as Rose discusses earthy tones.

911---NOT Noah.

Like a child hearing the ice cream truck, I jump up with my phone in hand. "Excuse me, I have an emergency call." I sprint to the door.

Rose offers a quick nod. "Of course. I hope all is well."

I push the phone icon before I'm halfway down the stairs and hear Wayne's voice after the first ring.

"Wayne? What's going on?"

"Carla. I didn't mean to scare you but I thought you'd want to know."

My heartbeat feels like it went off pace from acceleration and worry. "Who? If it isn't Noah, is it Will? Jenna? Sara?"

His voice is steady. "Your classmate. The woman I passed that day when I came to school to help you during that storm."

Ella.

My hand starts shaking. "Oh, no. Tell me everything." I march outside so Brandi won't hear until I have all the information.

"Zeke and I just finished a call and were leaving the hospital when another came in from outside of town. Woman, mid-thirties, fell down the basement stairs. Distal radius fracture, periorbital hematoma, lacerations was what we were told."

He could have heard my sigh without the phone. "Okay. Broken wrist, black eye, some cuts. Could be worse."

Wayne pauses. "There's something else, though."

"What?"

"We have reason to believe she didn't fall down the stairs. Or if she did, it wasn't an accident."

⧖⧖⧖

Ten minutes later everyone at the school is out the door and on their way to the hospital.

Daniel pulls out his phone. "I'm calling my dad to see if he's on ER duty."

"Good idea." I call out as I unlock my truck. "I'll check in with Jack Hunt. He's the sheriff. Maybe he knows something."

Sandy rides with me while Claire and Mitzi carpool with Daniel. Rose drives herself but follows me.

"Is Ella okay?" Sandy's voice is quiet.

"As far as survival, yes."

"Did her husband do this?"

I bite my lip as I make a hard right turn. "The paramedics suspect so."

"You might want to say another prayer." Sandy's words seem measured.

"How come?"

"'Cuz if I see that guy, I'm probably going to put a beat down on *him*."

Sandy's confession doesn't surprise me. Because the same feelings are bubbling up in me.

We barge into the ER lobby like a swarm of bees. Wayne steps out from the lounge area before I reach the registration desk. If he's upset about how I rejected a relationship with him, he doesn't show it.

I skid to a stop in front of him. "How is Ella?"

He rakes his hand through his wavy locks. "She came back from x-ray. I talked to Dr. Garrett about our suspicions. Jack's on his way."

"Good. How about her husband?"

166

Wayne rolls his eyes. "The guy's having a fit. He wants to be in the exam room with her."

Daniel joins us. "Of course he does."

I fold my arms. "How is he being handled while we wait for Jack?"

Wayne grins and looks to Daniel. "I hear your dad is Dr. Garrett. He's a great guy."

Daniel furrows his brow. "Thanks. What's he doing?"

"He discreetly called security. One of the best officers is suddenly in charge of registration and insurance. Mr. Traynor needs to fill out all the paperwork. If only our registration worker could do his job efficiently." Wayne winks.

I playfully hit him in the arm as Daniel and I chuckle. "Brilliant. Do you think we can see her?"

Wayne shrugs. "It's up to Doc Garrett." He gestures down the hall. "Here he comes now."

Daniel walks over to his dad while the rest of us hang back. After a couple minutes, Daniel waves me over.

"Dad, you remember Carla Rowling. Her son had the eye injury."

The man in the white coat and salt and pepper hair nods. "Hello. Your friend Ella had her arm wrapped. She told me her husband did it. I looked up her file and this isn't her first ER trip. I have her permission to call social services. But, she's jumpy. Carla, she's asking for you."

I exhale. "Okay. Can I go in now?"

"Yes. The social worker is on her way. Ella's mom is on her way to pick the kids up from school. I believe the plan is for Ella and the kids to go with her parents."

Claire steps up. "Is everything okay?"

Daniel puts his hand on her back. "Ella admitted her husband did it. A social worker is going to talk to her." He turns to his father. "Dad, this is Claire. The girl I told you about. Claire, my father, Dr. Garrett."

Claire extends her hand as Rose, Sandy and Mitzi join our circle. "I'm sorry I'm not meeting you under happier circumstances. Your son has done a wonderful job helping me."

The two Garrett men exchange looks. "I'm not surprised." The doctor glances at me. "Ready to see Ella?"

"Yes. Let's pray she doesn't change her mind."

With all my hospital visit experience I'm still in shock when I see Ella. Her arm bandaged tight past her elbow. Her right eye has a protective patch. Deep brown circles hang under her good eye. Green and purple marks dot her skin. The beautiful color job Claire created is a pile of black and red limp hair.

"Ella." My greeting is more of a cry.

A deep wail fills the room. "He hated my hair."

I rush over and pull up a chair as I reach for her good hand. "He won't stop. You know that, right?"

More sobs. "My kids."

"Your mom is getting them."

She shakes her head. Strands of black hair stick to her forehead. "They saw him hit me once. I don't want them to grow up this way."

I pat her damp tresses. "They won't. My friend Jack is on his way. So is the social worker. Tell them everything. For you. The kids."

Before she can reply, there's a knock on the door, and it opens.

"Ella? I'm Lisa Murray from social services, and Sheriff Hunt is with me. May we visit with you for a few minutes?"

She looks to me, her mouth still quivering.

"It's going to be okay."

Ella blinks back tears. "Come on in."

Forty-five minutes later I walk out, confident Ella's in good hands and that her husband won't be bothering her---at least not for the time being. Claire, Daniel, Sandy, Mitzi and Wayne stand and walk over.

"Rose sent her apologies. She had to pick up her daughter. How's Ella?" Claire asks.

I clear my throat. "Ella told Jack and the social worker everything. Once she's discharged, she plans to go to stay with her parents'. And get counseling."

Even Sandy smiles. Claire lets out a squeal.

Daniel pats my back. "We all make a great team."

I look to the floor before I lock eyes with Wayne. "Thank you for letting me know about Ella."

"No problem. Glad she's going to be okay." He pulls keys out of his front pocket. "Been a long day. I think I'll head home." He turns to the gang. "Take care." Wayne's focus returns to me. "See ya around, Carla." He opens his arms and without thinking, I step into his hug.

A deep, pained voice causes me to turn around. "Carla?"

"Will?"

Chapter Twenty-Four

Wayne nearly pushes me to the hospital floor and everyone backs away as if Will and I are contagious.

My voice sounds high-pitched. "What are you doing here?"

Will appears different. No hat. No plaid. No smile. "I've been trying to find you."

Wayne steps forward. "If you're here, where's Noah?"

"With Ben." Will doesn't even look at him. "I thought maybe you were working on hair stuff at school. Your teacher was there picking up some notes and told me you were here."

I bob my head like one of those desktop toys. "Right. We all were here because of Ella."

Please believe me. For once, I'm telling the truth.

Will glances toward the exit. "Can we talk?"

No one seems to have the courage to say anything. The lounge area feels more like a morgue. Without replying I reach for my purse and follow him to the door.

"Did you want to get something to eat? Talk in my truck? Oh, wait. I brought Sandy here. I might need to take her…"

Will stops on the sidewalk and speaks with confidence I've never heard from him before. "Carla, this won't take long. I promised Ben I'd pick up Noah so he wouldn't have to spend the night. That's why I'm here."

"Noah?" I can barely get his name out.

He shakes his head. "No. Us." He swallows and stuffs his hands into his pockets. "I know in Speculator Falls I'm good 'ole flannel-wearing Will.' Everyone thinks my life's a breeze and I don't have problems. Maybe I'm more easygoing than most."

"Will, you are loved." My voice breaks.

"I know. But for a romantic love that I want to last, there has to be trust."

My heart drops. "You can trust me. I've learned so much from how I treated you."

"Right. At my expense. Now I'll second guess everything you say." He glances back inside the ER. "And who you're talking to. Or hugging."

I wipe my eyes with my sleeve. "I was thanking him for calling about Ella. There's nothing between us. He knows that."

"I'm not sure I ever will. And I can't be with someone I don't trust." Now his voice cracks.

"Please, Will. Don't."

A couple tears fall onto his casual shirt. "I don't mean to put you in a tight spot but you should find someone else to watch Noah. I think it would be too hard. For him. For me."

"No. Please." If desperation has a pitch, I've hit it. I reach out but he steps back.

"I have to go. I won't say anything to Noah. I'll go home once I know you're back in town. Bye." His footsteps echo throughout the lot until I hear a thunderous shriek drown out his walk.

My sobs.

⧗⧗⧗

I drag myself out of bed and hit the pavement for a run before Betty even wakes. It's early enough the streetlights turn off and the sun starts its daylight shift. I've never run without sleep but that's where I'm at. Exhausted and in need of something that feels better than my broken heart.

The run helps me process. As I run down Main Street and circle back to Betty's I realize it's the middle of May. The danger of severe weather is over. I can commute to school and take care of Noah. It's a lot, but I wouldn't feel worse than I already do.

A male voice greets me at sunrise. "Carla? You're up early."

I stop in front of the bakery where Les carries a drink and a small brown bag. "Good morning. Trying to get a good run in before class."

He chuckles. "You make me feel bad. I'm up getting a coffee and a muffin."

"You have a full day teaching us. Enjoy that breakfast."

172

Les lifts the cup. "Plan to, thanks. And Carla? You're doing a tremendous job. I know cosmetology is a huge transition for you, but you're well on your way. I predict a bright future for you."

Again, the wooden sign Will and Noah made for me for my business comes to mind.

"That's kind of you to say. I have some challenges, but I'm determined." I blink moisture off my eyelashes. Not sure if it's perspiration or tears.

He pats me on the shoulder. "It shows. Keep rising up to those challenges. You're going to do just fine. I'll see you soon."

With a wave goodbye, I resume my jog. I love Will. I ache knowing I blew it. But Les is right. Deep down I know with God's help, I'm going to survive the mess I made.

⧖⧖⧖

The Gloversville Beauty School hovers around as soon as I walk to my desk. No one speaks for a few moments, but Sandy breaks the silence.

"Are you okay?"

I put down my backpack and muster a smile. "I will be. Not today, but in time." I swallow hard. "I know I left in a hurry last night. Will broke up with me."

Within seconds I'm surrounded by hugs. Daniel talks first. "That stinks, Carla. I'm really sorry."

When our eyes meet, I realize he's genuine.

Claire holds on a little longer. "What can we do to help? Do you want us to talk to him?"

I shake my head. "I don't think it would help. It's hard but I need to trust God with this. I'll be okay, really. My question is, how's Ella?"

Mitzi sighs. "She's really in pain today. Her mom's with her. Ella will need surgery on her wrist."

Ugh. That poor girl. "Is she changing her mind about her husband?"

Sandy chuckles. "No, and I don't think anyone would let her."

173

Rose pushes through the door holding a cardboard box. She rests it on the front table and dusts off her hands. "Okay, my friends, it's a busy day. Before we enter the world of facials and makeup, let's start with Ms. Traynor."

We scurry to our seats. I'm probably more interested in this topic than any other she'll mention today.

"I visited her this morning to bring her gifts on behalf of the school. She's doing well despite the ordeal but she plans on withdrawing from the school."

Claire gasps.

Rose coughs before continuing. "Ella needs surgery on her wrist and that prevents her from working the labs and with our clients. She wouldn't be able to take the exam. There's a lot for her to sort through within her family. They might move for a fresh start."

Mitzi raises her hand as if we're in elementary school. "What happens to her, though? Ella's done all this work. She's good."

Our instructor nods. "Sadly, Ella becomes one of the statistics I mentioned when we started. Not everyone graduates. Let's hope in her new transition she eventually finds her way back."

I look at the raised eyes and open mouths. "Hey, guys. Let's focus on the good news."

Daniel leans back in his chair. "Okay, I'll bite. What good news?"

"She's safe."

⧖⧖⧖

When I return to Betty's, I'm depleted. Wayne has Noah and that helps. With school, sadness about Ella leaving school and Will out of my life, I'm too tired to drive back home. Besides, I have to share the breakup news with Betty.

Like nearly every evening, she has dinner prepared before I put my things down.

Betty places a dish in front of my table setting. "Carla, I'm so glad you're here. You had a late night."

"Yes. A lot was going on." I scoop some salad into my bowl. "In fact, I have to talk to you."

Betty tilts her head and stops spooning out the corn. "I hope it isn't anything serious."

As scary as my future feels, I could be charting a new life like Ella with the issues she's dealing with. I place a piece of meatloaf on my dish and clear my throat. "Last night one of the students ended up in the hospital because of domestic abuse. She's going to be okay, but while I was there, Will showed up and saw me hugging Wayne." My voice catches as I remember the hurt look on Will's face.

"Oh, Carla. I'm so sorry."

"For Will it was the last straw. We broke up."

Betty covers her mouth with her hand for a moment, shaking her head. "Dear, that's terrible. How can I help?"

"I need to take care of Noah. Wayne has him tonight but the weather is better, there's no reason I can't commute to school from Speculator Falls. I think I need to make that change."

Betty sighs. "You have to leave here, don't you?"

I nod. "I've enjoyed living here. You have no idea what a blessing you are. I promise I'll pay through the end of the semester."

She waves her hand. "That's the last thing I'm worried about. I'm going to miss you. You don't know what a strong young woman you are."

"Thank you. I don't know about that, but this I do know. I'm finally learning how strong my God is."

The good news is I don't have a lot of studying nor a lot of packing to do. I finish both before dusk and am about to join Betty in the living room when the doorbell rings.

She hasn't had a visitor that I remember, especially at night. "Do you want me to get it?"

"Thanks, Carla. Probably a salesperson. They should keep better hours." She's focused on her television crime show.

I peek through the hole and realize the visitor is someone I know. Daniel.

Chapter Twenty-Five

Daniel grins as I swing the door open. "Hey. I was in the neighborhood?"

I gesture him inside. "You don't sound so sure. Everything okay?"

He takes a few steps inside. "I'm sorry to bother you. I guess I needed to process some things and you're good at that."

Daniel must be ill. He's never been so complimentary. "Okay, well come in. I can't remember if you've met Betty Cross yet. Betty, Daniel from school, is here. We're going to talk for a bit. Daniel, Betty."

He walks over to her before she can rise from her chair. "Hi, Miss Betty. I didn't mean to barge in so late."

"No problem, Daniel. It's good to have activity around here."

I look to the dining room table. "Did you want to talk in there?"

He nods and follows me. "Something happened tonight and I needed to bounce it off someone. You had something similar happen from what you shared, so here I am."

We take a seat across from each other. "Okay. Let's hear it."

"Carla, my dad called and asked to meet with me. He said he watched me last night with the whole Ella thing and thought I did a fantastic job handling myself. Dad said I had strong leadership skills and a friendly personality with the public."

Competitive Daniel in the classroom has his issues. But Dr. Garret's right. Daniel's done a wonderful job working with Claire and being supportive for Ella. He's even been compassionate toward me and my breakup with Will.

"It had to mean a lot to hear that from your Dad."

He nods. "That's not it, though. He offered to purchase or build me a salon once I receive my license."

Now I get why Daniel's here talking to me. It's a Howard Wheaton kind of gesture. "That's incredible! You must be so excited."

Daniel's face reads more like a man assigned to diffuse a bomb. "Shocked is more like it. Dad and I haven't seen eye to eye on much of anything. He told me that in a weird way, he sees the correlation between him practicing medicine and me working in cosmetology."

"Okay, I'll bite. What's similar between them? I guess some of our clients will feel like their appointment is life or death."

Laughter fills the room. "More like serving the community. Showing empathy. I was so insecure when school started, but I really believe in what I'm doing. To hear Dad agree, it's amazing."

I reach over and touch his forearm. "I'm glad, Daniel. As someone who didn't receive encouragement from my parents, it's a gift."

Daniel reaches into his pocket and pulls out a white cloth. "I doodled on a napkin. What Rose said in class makes sense." He pushes the napkin toward me. It looks like a salon sketch. "I know I want a salon in Lake George and to reach out and have year-round clients in Bolton Landing. Someplace that takes care of clients from head to toe."

I rotate the napkin and study his drawing. A full-service salon with a manicure/pedicure station. Waxing. Facials. Make-up area. A color lab of sorts where stylists could mix color, keeping files on client colors for reference. A welcome center with coffee and light refreshments. Situated on a walkway that faces the water with shops nearby.

"Daniel. This is amazing. A lot of work, but with the right people in place, you could be the talk of the Adirondacks. I'd certainly travel for that kind of pampering."

His eyes widen. "Really?"

"Absolutely. Lake George has a higher income bracket than most places around here. A lot of Albany folks are in the area for the summer. The other seasons might take some creative publicity, but you've got what it takes. Women love to feel special. You'd have everything under one roof."

He nods. "Great. I was hoping it made sense. So, what do you think about possibly being part of the team?

My laugh starts as a giggle but soon turns into a full-body cackle. When I glance at him, his expression is stoic. "Wait. You're serious?"

"Why not? We argued all year, but we're both good at what we do. That's what I want."

I start waving my hands. "No, not me. We'd hurt each other competing, first of all. It would also mean moving. I can't do that to Noah. The plan God has for me is to go back to Speculator Falls."

Daniel bites his lip for a moment and looks to his sketch. "You sure? There's a chair that could easily have your name on it."

I straighten. "I am. But you know, Claire's rocking the facials and make up. Why not ask her? You two seem to have a connection, anyway."

If he notices my grin, he doesn't say anything. "It crossed my mind. We haven't said anything, but we're kind of dating. I like her. A lot."

He seems clueless that his news would surprise no one at school.

"Good for you. Actually, you could bring on Mitzi and Sandy, too. They have been strong all year long. Sandy does the best waxing I've ever seen."

Now it's Daniel's turn to laugh. "Because she enjoys inflicting pain."

I roll my eyes. "Oh, stop. She's got an edge to her but she can reach a clientele you, Claire, Mitzi, and I never can. Once you get to know her you realize she's a softie."

"True. I know I have time before I can make it all happen, but I had to tell someone who understands. I feel so unworthy. I mean, this is a huge gesture."

Boy do I relate. "It is. Honestly, I blew it in a lot of ways because I felt so overwhelmed with the gift I was given. Instead of feeling unworthy, make a go of this. Give it everything you've got. You have what it takes."

Daniel stands and stretches. "It's going to be hard to focus on school work when I just want to get started."

I rise and walk toward the door. "As much as I'd love that so I can be number one cosmetologist, you need the license to realize the dream. We're getting there. You'll do fine."

"Thanks, Carla. Would you want to join me for lunch sometime when I ask Mitzi and Sandy to join me?"

I notice Claire's name isn't mentioned.

"Sure. Won't you invite Claire, too?"

He walks out and shrugs. "Of course. But, you know, I thought I'd ask her about her role in this privately."

If I can't have a happy ending, I'm thrilled Daniel seems to be on his way to one.

⧗⧗⧗

After Daniel leaves, I say goodnight to Betty and prepare for bed. I remember my phone battery is low so I walk out to the kitchen in my sweats in search of my purse. Once I find it, I retrieve my cell and head back to my room to plug it in and let it charge. There's a blinking light so I turn the screen on to see what the notification is.

A text.

Wayne.

Carla, call me when you get this. Noah's in trouble.

Chapter Twenty-Six

Not even a tanker of coffee from those big mugs at the gas station helps me feel awake as I make my way back to Speculator Falls in the early morning. Betty didn't want me to travel late at night, upset, when nothing could really be resolved until morning. As wise as her advice was, I didn't sleep. Wayne's conversation kept replaying through my mind.

"Carla, I'm sorry to bother you but I figured you'd want to know."

"Is Noah okay? Did he get hurt? Was there another explosion?"

There's a small laugh on the other side of the phone. "Well, not like the last time. He's suspended."

If I didn't know Wayne's voice so well, I would have been certain that he had the wrong number.

"Suspended? Noah?"

"He hit a kid. Anyway, Will's name was on the file, you know, because of you being gone, so the school called him first. He called me."

This gets better and better.

"Okay. So what do we do?"

"The principal wants us there at nine in the morning to discuss everything."

I rake my hand through my limp hair. "Alright. I packed up anyway, so I'll load the truck and head home. I'll meet you both at the school at nine."

Before I reach the school, I stop at home to unload the truck. As I walk through the kitchen and put my few boxes on the table, it feels empty without Will. The living room and the video games he played with Noah. The kitchen and how he'd help me cut vegetables for salad. The garage and the sign he made for my future salon. So many memories. But there's no time to grieve. I have a son suspended from school.

⧖⧖⧖

Wayne and Noah are already in the reception area when I arrive. I take a deep breath as I walk over.

My voice is flat and unemotional. "I'd like to know what happened."

Wayne leans forward. "He was in lunch when…"

I hold up my hand. "No. I want to hear it from Noah."

My son keeps his gaze on the floor. "Dad's right. I was at lunch. Todd was bothering Brittany. She asked him to stop. He didn't. I asked him to stop. He didn't. I told him to stop. He didn't. He pushed me, and Brittany was close enough that she fell. And I slugged him and gave him a black eye."

Any pit I had in my stomach from losing Will and knowing Noah was suspended is now the size of the Grand Canyon. Thirteen and suspended. Because of a girl.

"Okay. Wayne, what did the principal say?"

He rolls his eyes. "That the school has a zero tolerance policy for violence, blah, blah, blah."

I tilt my head and examine Wayne's expression. "I'm sorry, I don't understand. Why are you saying blah?"

Wayne stands and moves closer while I take a step back. "Carla, he protected the girl and shut down a bully. Way I see it, he's a hero."

My mouth forms a circle as words fail me for a few moments.

"He hit someone."

Noah shakes his head. "I know, I know. I messed up. I don't want to talk about it, though. Let me deal with the punishment."

I don't even notice I'm pacing. "We have to talk about it. That's the purpose of this meeting." I narrow my eyes and direct them at Wayne. "And it's important we be on the same page. Hero is not a word I think anyone else is going to throw around in the principal's office."

Before he can reply, footsteps enter the reception area.

"Good morning. Can I help you, sir?" The receptionist asks.

"Actually, the people I want to see are over there."

I gasp as soon as I hear the voice and turn. "Will?"

There's still no plaid shirts or orange hunting hats. He's wearing jeans that look new and a white shirt that accents his biceps. It's so tempting to stare.

Wayne's sigh is a tad louder than it needs to be.

Noah springs out of his chair. "Will! What are you doing here?"

Will saunters over and stands next to Noah. "The school called me first. I wanted to make sure Wayne got my message. I was afraid maybe no one would come to the meeting. So, I decided to make sure."

There, in the middle of the school office lobby, I realize I'm madly in love with Will. Not just because he's fun to be with and is good with Noah. He's the most caring man I've ever known.

Wayne shrugs. "Yep, got the message. We're all set here."

I was less nervous dealing with a bear call as sheriff. "Will, thank you. It's above and beyond and Noah and I really appreciate it."

The principal's door opens and a short man with a wide tie and a bad comb-over stands at the threshold. "Noah Rowling?"

Noah pauses before moving toward the door. "Thanks, Will. Pray for me."

Will smiles and pats him on the shoulder as Noah walks past. "I promise."

Wayne turns and follows Noah without speaking. My legs feel like cement blocks. Is it because I dread this meeting or I don't want to leave Will?

"Thank you again, Will."

He nods and turns to the exit. "Noah's a good kid, Carla."

My heart races faster than horses out of the gate at the Kentucky Derby. "Thank you. I'm afraid. I don't want him to repeat my mistakes."

"You're an excellent mom. I'm praying. Bye, Carla."

When he leaves, I'm pretty sure a piece of me goes with him.

⧗⧗⧗

When the door closes, it sounds like the clang of the jail cell. The man thrusts out his hand. "Lloyd Drivnell, acting principal. I've been here since Mrs. Miller retired."

Wayne returns the handshake first. "Wayne Peterson."

I look the administrator in the eye. "Carla Rowling, Noah's mom."

The man nods and gestures for us to take the trio of seats across from the desk. "There was some confusion when we tried to contact you." He looks to Wayne. "Mr. Peterson, you weren't listed as a contact at all." Then he glances toward me. "And Ms. Rowling, the first contact wasn't you. It was Will Marshall, the man who delivers our food supplies."

Noah keeps his focus on the floor. I'd like to do the same.

I clear my throat. "Yes. I've been away during the week for cosmetology school. Will is a trusted friend who agreed to be his caregiver. However, with the weather improving, I'm able to commute now, so I'm the first contact. I forgot to make the change with the office." Because it just happened.

"I see. Well, perhaps that explains some of this trouble." Mr. Drivnell pushes up on the bridge of his glasses with his pointer finger.

"I'm sorry?"

He opens a red folder and spreads out some papers. "Noah's been a model student until this year. Isn't that when you left home for school and had Mr. Marshall take over? Wayne's mouth opens, but nothing comes out.

I don't have the same trouble. "Yes, but---"

"And isn't it recent that you, Mr. Peterson, entered Noah's life?"

Wayne nods.

"That's a lot of upheaval for a young man, don't you think?"

Oh, this guy. I narrow my eyes and try to steady my breathing. "We aren't the first non-traditional family to enter these school doors."

He chuckles. "No, but you are here for a violent crime and statically those take place when home life is volatile. It's a theory, nothing to get upset about. I just noticed he's never had trouble until now."

Suddenly Noah springs to life. "Todd was bothering Brittany. He wouldn't stop."

Wayne shoots Noah a look and gestures for him to sit.

Drivnell shuffles the papers. "Right. And Brittany is your girlfriend, correct?"

Noah sighs. "Yes."

"And you're thirteen?"

My pulse is higher than anyone at Woodstock was. "Mr. Drivnell, can we keep theories out of it and talk about what really happened and what an appropriate punishment is?"

"Of course. Although the numbers say teens who are romantically involved too soon are more susceptible to be teen parents. I'm trying to look at this picture as a whole and stop the slide I think is ready to take place."

Now I'm out of my seat, shaking with fury. "Where is the other boy and his family? Is he getting punished?"

"Yes, but let's be real. Noah made a threat and threw the first punch. We take that very seriously."

Noah stands next to me. "Do I get to say anything?"

We all speak at once. "No!"

Mr. Drivnell closes the folder. "I don't think there is anything more to say. A week suspension, minus one day already served. Thank you, everyone." With that, he stands and shows us the door.

"Thanks for your time." Wayne shakes his hand but I march past the principal, Noah not far behind me.

"Carla. Wait." Wayne jogs in order to meet us at the front door.

I hold the metal bar so the entrance is ajar. I feel a breeze clothed in the scent of oncoming rain dance past me. "What?"

"This doesn't define Noah's future. Don't let it get to you."

We walk to the visitor lot. I'm tempted to pick up the pace and keep running.

Noah kicks at pebbles. "Drivnell is a jerk. He wouldn't even listen."

Wayne nods. "He's just a pencil pusher. The guy doesn't even know how to work with kids."

Or parents. But that's beside the point.

"Are you two finished? He's an authority figure. Noah, his name is Mr. Drivnell. And his bottom line is the same as every school. There is zero tolerance for violence. The damage has been done. Now it's time to pay the consequences. It's too late for me to go back to beauty school today, so Noah, come with me. Wayne, I'll call you later so we can figure this out."

Now he takes a turn kicking at a small rock. "Right."

The truck is close enough I click the key fob to unlock it. Noah starts for the passenger side, but stops. "Thanks, Dad, for coming."

Wayne smiles and gives him a side hug and pat on the shoulder. "We'll get through this, son." He glances at me as I open the driver side and climb in.

"I'll be in touch." I shut the door and face my teen. "What on earth were you thinking, hitting someone?"

His eyes narrow. "I would've asked for advice, but you're never around." With that, he turns to the window and blocks me out.

The two of us are in a shouting match before we were even out of the lot. I didn't pay attention to our destination, I have the vehicle in drive and my foot on the gas. My mind and mouth are on auto-pilot.

"Noah, talk to me. How many nights did I spend telling you that violence is never the answer?"

He shifts, crosses his arms, and looks ahead, jaw tight.

"I want an answer."

A hot breath of air fills the truck cab. "I don't get why you're freaking out. You heard Dad. What I did was heroic. Brittany was in trouble."

Great. Side with Wayne. "Noah, I get it. But you know the drill. Get an adult if you're in trouble. Now this is on your school file. You have all that work to make up. On top of that, you have a reputation. Do you know how long that takes to erase?"

The road's familiar but it's as if the truck is driving itself.

He spits his words out and targets my heart. "No, but you do."

I turn to him long enough to shoot a glare as sharp as daggers. "What does that mean?"

"You aren't mad at me. You're angry at Mr. Drivnell because he basically blamed my choice on you. All his statistics were digs at you, and you let him."

Drops hit the windshield, enough to turn on the wipers.

"That's not true."

Fat, wet splats cover the windows in a dump that doesn't seem like it has an end. I look to the right and realize where I am. The senior center. I pull in the lot and the rain accompanies our rhythm of words I'm already starting to regret.

"Mom. You don't want me to be around Brittany or any girl. Face it. You think I'm going to get some girl pregnant. Just like Dad did with you."

I try to open my mouth but the pain deep inside weakens my resolve.

"And what he said about your schedule has to be bugging you. I never got in a fight before you went to school. He insinuated your dreams ruined me. I'm just a kid who saw someone he cares about in a bad situation, and I tried to help her. You're making this way more than it is because of Drivnell."

"Noah, you have no idea what it's like to earn a label and have it follow you everywhere. I'm trying so hard to protect you from making the mistakes I've made." I look to the window thinking it must be open for so much moisture to come in and wet my face. It's not the rain.

His tone sounds desperate and sad. "Every time you say that, I feel like I am a mistake to you. It drives me crazy. I need some air. I'll walk the rest of the way." The door opens and slams before I can respond.

I also exit. "Noah! C'mon, it's pouring!"

He's running faster than I ever have.

I lean on the hood and grieve for all that I've done, thought and said. Noah threw truth about me I never dared to ponder.

A door opens, followed by footsteps. "Carla? You okay?"

The masculine voice that is like an umbrella in rain to me walks closer.

I lift my head to face him. "Will. Noah's furious with me. He ran home."

He flaps his arms around and pulls on his clothing. The rain is blinding enough I can't quite see what he's up to until I feel his touch. "Here, have my rain jacket. Let's get inside. Jenna will hurt you if you get sick before the wedding."

I let out a half-laugh-half sob and allow him to guide me through the front door, wishing I could turn back time and make everything okay with Noah, and everything permanent with Will.

Chapter Twenty-Seven

The fork clangs and chatter cease as soon as Will escorts me inside the senior center. I shake my hair and hear drops fall onto the floor. Jenna steps out from her office, her eyes wide.

"Carla? What happened?"

Will steps back as Jenna moves in. Before I can blink, he's gone. Probably back to work.

"Noah and I had a terrible fight, and he ran home. He's suspended. The principal made a few cracks that hit close to home, and Noah called me on it."

Jenna shakes her head. "Wow. How much am I missing with this wedding? I can't imagine him in trouble." She gestures me to follow her, walks to her office and offers me a seat.

"He hit a kid."

She gasps.

"Because of Brittany."

Now she's cracking a smile. "Well, there you go. I see why you're upset."

I twist my hair and squeeze out a couple more drops of water. "It's all too much. Trying to go to school. The principal insinuated my not being around is why Noah's acting up. He didn't need to say that, I thought about it the whole drive home. I miss Will so much I ache. I hurt, Jenna. I've made such a mess of things. Noah isn't the only one that would like to run."

She pulls a chair next to me. "I love you, girl. But can I ask a tough question?"

I shrug. "Why not? I couldn't possibly feel worse."

Jenna gently holds my arm. "Don't you think it's time you stop running?"

⧗⧗⧗

The charred smell of a burned pot and vegetable soup greets me as Noah remains silent. I drop my purse on the floor and shuffle over to the kitchen table where he's stirring the bowl, but not eating.

I pull up a chair across from him. "We need to talk."

He looks up, and his hair bobs into his eyes. "I know." His voice is almost a whisper.

My own sound isn't much stronger. "Noah, will you forgive me?"

He tilts his head and squints. "For what? I'm the one that got suspended and stormed off."

I nod. "You're a lot wiser than I give you credit for. I've projected a lot of fears from my life onto you, and it isn't fair. You're absolutely right about me not wanting girls around. I'm afraid. The last thing I want to do is have you think that you are a mistake. But at the same time, I want to make sure you understand the consequences of becoming a teen parent. It was hard in a lot of ways. I never want you to have to fight for the many things I had to as a young mom. I never communicated that well to you, and I'm sorry."

Noah drops the spoon into his bowl. "You're an amazing mom. I don't tell you that enough. I shouldn't have hit Todd. I'm sorry."

"I appreciate that you respect women, I do. We'll get through this suspension and move forward. The good news is, you have facts that I didn't at your age."

Noah shrugs. "What's that?"

"God promises that each day is a new start. Something I haven't chosen to believe. You got in a fight and broke the rules. That doesn't mean you're a troublemaker. I had a baby when I was in high school. That doesn't mean I'm rebellious or any of the adjectives I heard over the years. What I am is blessed." I stand up, and Noah does the same. I walk over and give him a hug that he doesn't let go of right away. "Because I have you. If God's plan is just the two of us, I thank Him for that."

Noah steps back. "What if God's plan includes someone else in your life?"

The thought of Will in our lives gives me the chills. "I'd never take that person or the wonderful life I have for granted."

☒☒☒

Noah offers me some soup, and we enjoy our meal. After we finish, I decide to call Betty.

She picks up on the second ring. "Hello? Carla?"

"Hi, Betty. I wanted to check in and see how you're doing." I rinse my bowl and place it in the sink.

There's a light chuckle on the other end of the phone. "Me? I don't have anything going on to share. I'm bored. It's you that I want to hear an update from. How's Noah? How are you?"

"He's suspended for a few days but we're okay. I need to figure out a plan while I'm at school, but God's got this." I wink at Noah. "God's got us."

I can almost see Betty's smile. "I have an idea. You two stay here. Noah can help me while you're at school. There are some easy handyman projects he could handle."

Actually, that's not a bad idea.

"Are you sure?"

"Certain."

"Betty, you're an answer to prayer."

⧗⧗⧗

Noah's suspension passes quickly thanks to Betty's hospitality. Those two bond as he hangs pictures, plants annuals, and cleans her garage. She has a new stomach to feed and Noah's more than a willing snacker. When class dismisses for the weekend, and it's time to return to Speculator Falls, I'm sad to separate the two.

"Mom, why doesn't Miss Betty come home with us?"

I look over at her. "Betty? We don't have anything exciting going on this weekend but you're more than welcome to join us."

There's a beautiful twinkle in her eyes. "Try and stop me. Thank you. I love being with both of you."

Thirty minutes later we cram into the truck and are headed north. We're almost in Northville when my phone rings.

Jenna.

I push the "talk" button on the dashboard and hear her stressed voice.

"Tell me you're on your way to Speculator Falls."

A week before her wedding, I'm surprised she hasn't called more often.

"I am. I have Noah and Betty with me."

There's muffled voices in the background before she responds. "I need a gigantic favor from you." She stretches out the word "gigantic."

"What's going on?"

"My sister Meg surprised me by coming a few days early. I thought she was traveling with my parents, but she came on her own. Her car is full of cookies for the wedding."

I slow down for bicyclists ahead. "Okay. What's the problem?"

"I don't have room to store them and Ben's freezer is broken. Only one person has a deep freezer that can hold all the goodies my mom made for the wedding." "So, what do you need me for?"

"Because Will's still on delivery and he told me you have a key to his place. Would you mind going to his house and helping Meg store all the cookies in his freezer?"

Okay, let myself into his house and fill his deep freezer. It's not the worst favor.

"What makes this errand so gigantic?"

There's a pause before she confesses. "Because he said he's on his last run of the day, and he'll go straight home. Chances are you two will be unloading cookies."

Chapter Twenty-Eight

Meg Anderson is a blonder, slightly taller version of her big sister, Jenna. She greets me in Will's driveway with three wrapped foil pans.

"Hey, Carla. From bridal shower to cookie hauler, right? We have our work cut out for us. My mom made enough cookies to feed everyone in the Adirondacks, not just the wedding guests." She laughs and hands me the pans before diving into her trunk to pick up three more trays.

I balance the pans on my knee as I hold Will's key. "Wow. How long has she been baking?"

Her shoulder length hair swings as she marches to his front door. "Don't even get me started. When Jenna announced the wedding wasn't going to be in Ohio, Mom was a little hurt. Then she decided she'd do the next best thing and bring Youngstown to Speculator Falls. So, she became a one-woman wedding cookie table creator."

I move forward so I can unlock the door, pushing away all the memories of times we watched movies, sat on the porch, or took our time when I had to say goodbye. "My son and a friend are with me, we can have this car unloaded in no time." With the cookie trays on the porch, I work the knob, twisting the key until the door opens. I gesture for Betty and Noah to come over as I pick up the pans and head inside.

"So, Jenna said the guy who lives here is your ex-boyfriend. Why do you have a key?"

She doesn't waste any time with pleasantries.

I turn on the light for the basement and take careful steps down until I reach the freezer. "It's pretty recent. I didn't think of returning the key, to be honest. We're still friends."

She places her cookies in the cold and faces me. "That's so weird. When my boyfriend broke up with me…" Her voice trails and she looks to the floor. "Anyway, let's get back to the car. I'd love to unload so I can drive to Ben's and see him and my sister."

Something tells me Meg has a lot of catching up to do with Jenna.

After a couple treks to the basement, the four of us meet at my vehicle for another round of tray-to-freezer delivery. I hand Noah a couple pans when I hear the crunch of gravel from tires.

Noah glances my way. "Will's here."

"It's okay. Really. Keep carrying cookies. He's had a long day."

Betty, Noah and Meg exchange looks, but Noah shrugs and the trio trots back inside to the basement.

Will waves and ambles over to the truck. "Hey, Carla. I see you got in the house okay."

I smile and reach for another pan. "I did. Thanks for letting us borrow your freezer." Looking up, his brown work shirt accents his green eyes, leaving a flutter in my stomach.

"No problem. Can I help? Looks like you guys tackled a lot of it already."

I shake my head. "No, you relax. You've had a busy day. We're almost done."

He jangles his keys. "You sure? I'm happy to help."

That's what makes him so adorable. "I insist. I'd give you a cookie but Meg would probably tell Jenna and I don't want to face those consequences." My giggle comes out naturally, and it's refreshing to hear his baritone chuckle.

He walks ahead of me and opens the door, watching me as I come closer. His stare takes me off guard, and my hands start to shake. The tray tilts, wobbling as if it were at the epicenter of an earthquake.

He lunges forward and puts his hands under the foil, touching mine. "You okay?"

My nerves spill out with more laughter. "Yes, close call. I'm not paying attention. Thanks for the save." I pass him and head into the house. "Now, go rest. We've got this."

Even as I walk down the stairs and place the treats in the freezer, my hands are still warm from Will's touch.

Betty pats my arm. "You okay?"

"Sure. Why?"

"Your cheeks are several shades pinker than normal."

☒☒☒

Meg's early arrival turbo boosts Jenna's wedding barometer. With less than a week to go, most of my non-school time is spent with the sisters and Sara. There's not enough coffee to keep me as wide eyed as Jenna.

She starts pacing around the home she rents from Sara. "The flowers. I forgot to order them. We don't have any for the wedding."

Sara chuckles. "Relax. Don't you remember I said months ago I'd take care of flowers? They'll be arriving Friday night. Enough for the entire wedding party and for decorating the church."

Jenna exhales. "Oh, thank goodness. I'm forgetting everything. I can't even find the clipboard Shirley gave me to keep track."

Meg tapes up another box that's headed to Ben's house. "That's what we're here for."

"Everything is in good shape. One week and you'll be walking down the aisle, marrying my grandson." Sara's face glows.

Meg stacks the box on top of the others. "So---what's the plan for this place once you leave here and move in with Ben?"

Jenna and Sara exchange looks, and Sara shrugs. "I haven't thought about it. I was so excited about the wedding, I forgot this house will be empty."

Meg nods as she wraps a figurine in newspaper. "Would you consider renting to me?"

The bride-to-be freezes. "Meg? You're moving here?"

"I'm thinking about it. Why not? I'm job hunting. I have my degree. I can get certified in New York, no problem."

Jenna furrows her brow. "This is a huge transition. Trust me. Then there's mom and dad. What are they going to say?"

She shrugs. "Not much. I'm twenty-two. You left and they survived."

Sara and I watch their interactions like a tennis match.

Jenna's jaw looks pretty tight. "Yes, but you're the baby. Don't you think this will crush them?"

Meg keeps boxing items without giving any of us a second glance. "I'm an adult. They knew we'd move on and out. It's time."

Jenna puts her hands on her hips and narrows her gaze, not that Meg has a clue. "Okay. I have to ask. What does Johnny think of all this?" Meg finally stops and faces her sister. "We're done. Which reminds me," She focuses on me. "How finished are you and Will Marshall? I could get lost in those green eyes, you know?"

Chapter Twenty-Nine

Walking down the sanctuary aisle to my seat, I realize next time I'm in the church I will be wearing a bridesmaid dress. Suddenly all the jokes Jenna made about a double wedding flood back, and a new wave of regret hits.

Then I turn and see Will sitting with Meg, and now the tidal wave is nausea.

"Hey, Carla." Will stands and starts holding out both hands, then quickly extends one for a handshake.

"Will. Good morning. Ready for a wedding?"

His face pales.

"You know, Ben and Jenna's?" What did he think? Him and Meg? Ugh.

I'm trying, Lord, but that would be asking too much of me right now.

He lets out a nervous laugh. "Right. Yes, I'd say I'm ready. Ben, he could be in a tux and down the aisle in ten minutes."

Meg suddenly stands and giggles a little louder than needed.

I manage a smile for his sake. "I believe it. Well, I better find my seat."

Will shuffles over, stepping on Meg's foot. "You could sit here. If you want."

Meg hops on one foot, biting her lip.

"No, I couldn't, I don't think there's enough room. Thanks, though." I sprint to my seat, my heart pounding.

Thanks, God. Even if Will and I never reunite, I'm thankful we can be kind to each other.

It takes me until the sermon before I can calm my thoughts and focus. Pastor Craig approaches the podium and opens his Bible.

"You know what I love about the Bible? It repeats the same theme over and over without getting boring. There's Paul and his journey when he was Saul. Rahab and her line of business, yet she is remembered as a woman of faith. One of my favorites is Zacchaeus. Can you guess the theme?"

Kyle Swarthmore is the first to shout out. "Short people?"

Chuckles fill the sanctuary.

"No, although the song mentions several times that Zacchaeus wasn't winning any height contests. The theme is that everyone's redeemable. Isn't that reassuring?"

I close my eyes for a moment, drinking in his statement.

"Zacchaeus wasn't a popular guy. He bought his way into a job as chief tax collector and took from the Jews to give to Rome. Not only that, he skimmed off the collection plate to help himself. It's safe to say he wasn't someone with a lot of friends. Perhaps that's what drew him to Jesus."

I look to the cross that hangs behind Pastor Craig. What's the connection between a crooked tax collector and our Savior?

"Although Jesus drew crowds of hungry people desperate for a touch from Him, there were people intent on getting Him to make a mistake. He was hated. And that was something Zacchaeus could relate to. When this short, chief tax collector hears Jesus is coming, he's a lot like the woman with the issue of blood. She was desperate enough for healing that she was willing to touch the hem of His garment if that was all she could get. Zacchaeus climbed a tree to get a glimpse of Christ. Do you think that's a position a man with his job would want to be seen in? A tree?"

Jenna nods as she takes notes.

"That's the power of Christ. When you no longer care how you look to the world because the desire to be near Him is that great, He'll meet you there. Not only does Jesus call Zacchaeus out of the tree, He lets Zacchaeus know He's heading to his house. The hated tax man. It was a bold move from Jesus and a message of hope for Zacchaeus."

It's such an inspiring passage of Scripture I can almost picture the man sliding down the sycamore tree to run home.

Pastor Craig flips a couple pages in his Bible. "If you're following along, this story is in Luke, chapter nineteen. And as you can imagine, the crowds aren't thrilled with Jesus and His dinner plans. They accuse Him of getting cozy with a crook, and Zacchaeus is probably in a panic. But he tells Jesus he's giving away half his earnings to the poor, and if he's doing anything wrong, he'll pay four times the amount." Pastor looks out to the congregation. "Remember---he was cheating the Jews and Rome and now, he's ready to make it right. He's proclaimed it to the crowds, but it's a promise he's made to Jesus. Zacchaeus is sold out for Christ and Jesus feels the same for the little man. I love this because if Jesus can redeem Zacchaeus, there's hope for us."

The chat Noah and I had earlier in the week reminds me of the sermon. I'm forgiven for my high school sin. And for all the waffling I did between Wayne and Will. And for taking Will for granted. Even in my lowest place, I'm still redeemable.

Jenna leans in and whispers, "You okay?"

I nod, forgiveness and love welling up and spilling over.

Pastor Craig walks away from the podium and to the center of the stage. "If you can relate to the Zacchaeus in the beginning---the desperate man willing to lower himself in the world's eyes by climbing a tree to see Jesus, there's a place for you at the altar. My prayer is no one leaves today the same. Let Christ's redemption touch you today. If anyone would like to come forward for prayer, you're invited."

Once again I rise, this time because I want to give thanks for my redemption. No matter what my future holds, I know I'm forgiven and loved. I stand up front without paying attention to the others. A streak of red walks by before I close my eyes, and I glance over.

Noah's come forward for prayer.

Standing right next to him is Will.

⏳⏳⏳

Twenty minutes later, Pastor Craig dismisses us and I feel like I could fly out of the sanctuary. It's a spiritual high blended with the wonder of feeling God's true love for me despite my choices and seeing Noah walk forward for prayer.

Ben catches me on the way to the lobby. "Carla, did you and Noah want to come out to the house for lunch?"

He's come a long way with his hospitality since falling in love with Jenna.

"I wish I could. I have a lot of studying to do. Once you guys are back from your honeymoon, we'll get together."

He breaks out into a grin at the mention of "honeymoon."

Jenna walks over and puts her arm around Ben. "What's so funny?"

I wink at him. "Ben giggles every time someone talks about your honeymoon."

Neither lovebird can respond because Will zig zags through the crowd and stands next to me.

"Hey, everyone. Carla, do you have a minute?"

My smile falls with my confidence. "Sure?"

"Great. The church library is quiet. Is that okay?"

I nod and try to read Jenna's expression, but she mouths, "I don't know."

Will leads the way and looks back as we walk, probably to make sure I'm still there. With each step I'm trying to figure out what's going on. When we reach the musty smelling room with books dating back to the 1950's, he turns on the light and stands inches away.

I swallow in an effort to find moisture for my throat. "Everything okay?"

"I hope so. This might seem dumb to you, and I don't want it to sound arrogant, but I have to say it."

He's blinking so much that I wonder if his message is in Morse code.

"You can talk to me. Go ahead."

He looks up and then to me. "Okay. Here goes. I forgive you."

I try to gauge his motivation by gazing deep in his eyes. The longer I look, the feeling from church returns. He means it. And it isn't condescending at all. "Will, it isn't necessary. I acted like a middle schooler and hurt you."

He takes another step forward, closing the gap between us. "I'm not done, though. I didn't handle your confession well, or anything after that. Would you consider forgiving me?"

Chapter Thirty

Even during the commute to school, I replay my conversation with Will. My normal reaction would have been to keep him and everyone but Noah at arm's length.

I fold my arms. "I'll forgive you on one condition."

Will's eyebrows arch. "Okay. What?"

"That you excuse me for my many failings with you. I've done a lot of soul searching and repenting for a lot of things. I completely took you for granted. You are a wonderful man. You always were."

He clears his throat. "I've been praying a lot. You didn't deserve my silent treatment or judgment. I'm really sorry."

The two of us stand there, forgiven.

Will clears his throat as I look at the ceiling.

"So…" He chuckles.

"What now?" I risk looking in the eyes of the man I love so much.

He opens his arms. "Can we start with a hug?"

I nearly jump into his embrace.

Start. I love that.

My heart still feels light and full of God's love when I enter the beauty school doors.

⧖⧖⧖

During afternoon break, Daniel takes the chair next to me and turns it so he sits backwards in it, facing me. "Doing anything tonight?"

I narrow my eyes and give a teasing grin. "I thought you were dating Claire."

He rolls his eyes. "I'm not asking you on a date. In fact, the gang is going if you want to."

"Going where?" I place my hands on my hips. "And thanks for thinking of me last."

"We're going to visit Ella for a few minutes. Then, I have somewhere I want to take you all."

I take out my phone and pull up my calendar app. "If you don't mind people coming with me. Wayne dropped my son off at Betty's house before work. I was going to take Betty and Noah out to dinner before I return to Speculator Falls."

Daniel drummed the desk. "Hmm. I don't want you out too late. But what I have to show you is really cool."

The intrigue gets to me. "I don't have any studying to do and Noah stays up, anyway."

He slaps the table. "Awesome. Meet at the pizza place at six? We'll grab a quick bite before going to see Ella."

"Do I get a hint?"

Daniel laughs and returns to his desk. "You're funny."

⧗⧗⧗

Ella's mom opens the door and smiles. "Hello, everyone. Come in."

Mitzi, Sandy, Betty, Noah, Daniel, Claire and I shuffle into the brick foyer.

Daniel speaks first. "Thanks for letting us visit. How's she doing?"

The silver-haired woman gestures for us to follow her. "Why don't you go see? The kids are with their grandpa so it's nice and peaceful. Take all the time you want."

We walk down the hall to the living room where Ella's reclining on the couch. She slowly sits up as soon as she sees us.

Mitzi enters first and walks over first to give her a hug. "You look great."

"No, I don't, but thank you. Each day I feel better. Please, sit down."

Noah and I remain standing, but I move a little closer. "Ella, this is my son, Noah, and my friend, Betty. Guys, this is Ella."

They exchange hello's and then I bend down and reach for her hand. "How are you, emotionally? Is there anything we can do to help?"

Ella bites her lip. "It's going to take time. But for the kids, I'm ready. My parents said we can stay as long as we need. The children are confused, but relieved, I think. There was so much tension. Dad took them to dinner and the movies to help them build trust in men. Things were volatile for so long..." Her voice trails off.

Sandy jumps in to squash the awkward silence. "Will you ever go back to school?"

Ella picks at a loose piece on the couch. "I don't know. I have to take things a day at a time. I liked it. I have a lot to consider."

Daniel stands. "I'm looking into opening a comprehensive salon in Lake George. It's not a done deal, but if plans come together and you and your family want a fresh start, you would be a great asset."

Betty clasps her hands together. "That sounds wonderful."

Ella nods. "Daniel, I have no doubt you'll make it happen. And if that's where I'm meant to be, you can bet I'll be licensed and ready to go."

⧗⧗⧗

After we leave Ella, Daniel hands me a slip of paper.

"What's this?"

His grin is wide. "The address where I'm going next to show you the surprise." He walks to his vehicle, whistling, as Claire, Mitzi, and Sandy climb in.

I hand the paper to Noah, and he plugs it into his phone. A map pops up, and Noah nudges me. "Hey, Mom. It's the library."

What is so important to Daniel at the library?

Betty offers a guess from the back seat as she clicks the seatbelt. "Maybe he found books that would help you all with school?"

I glance at Noah for his reaction, but he's on the phone typing so fast that I expect to see smoke rising up. Suddenly he lifts his head and looks at me. "Mom, we have to go home."

His face is expressionless but his chest is heaving.

"What's going on?"

"I have to get back to Speculator Falls. Something happened."

His phone keeps beeping through the vocalized map directions and when I look over, he's typing with mad force.

I try to think of all the things that would warrant a fast return. "Is someone hurt? Is it Ben and Jenna? The store?"

Noah drops the phone and bangs his fist against the door. "Brittany's at Frosty's sitting with Eric. Josh says it looks romantic."

⧗⧗⧗

It takes all of five minutes to pull into the library lot and spot Daniel and the girls.

I place the car in park and face Noah. "Give me a couple minutes, Bud. I'll let them know and we'll head home."

He nods, punching his seat.

I whisper a quick prayer and run over to the gang. "Hey, Daniel. I'm sorry, but I have to go."

He furrows his brow. "Everything okay?"

I shrug. "To a thirteen-year-old boy, no. I think it's important I be with him. You better text me the news."

Daniel smiles. "I can do better than that. I'll send you the link."

With that cliffhanger, I sprint back to the truck and shift. I glance at Noah. He's texting. I look at Betty in the mirror.

"So, Betty, do you want to come with us?"

She pats Noah on the shoulder. "I'd love that. And don't you two worry. I'm sure it's a miscommunication." Her smile could disarm warring nations.

Noah grips the phone and shakes it. "Mom, they're holding hands. What do I do?"

I turn onto the highway and sigh. Back in my school days the girls wrote notes to each other to process their drama. I have no idea what boys need. "What are you thinking about doing?"

He shakes his head. "Well, pound Eric for starters." Noah chuckles and sits up. "Kidding. Kind of. I don't know. If Brittany is out in public with him, I mean, what about me?"

Lord, please comfort Noah. And give me wisdom.

He squirms in the seat for a second before looking my way. "Mom, can I ask a question?"

I keep my eyes on the road, but nod. "Of course. Anything."

Noah holds up his phone. "Is it okay if I call Will?"

Chapter Thirty-One

I shake the ibuprofen bottle and it sounds near empty, and that only accelerates my stress headache. Noah's broken heart looms over the house like a rain cloud. He didn't say much after his chat with Will, but Noah confirmed after school that Brittany indeed found someone new even though she had feelings for Noah. My heart hurts for my son and my head spins.

Should I call Will for advice, too?

There's no time because the wedding rehearsal dinner is a day away and I'm still commuting to school. Jenna's busy with her family in town but I want to be there for her. And I'm not.

Daniel has no trouble reminding me I'm failing to be there for him, too. "Did you get my text?"

I barely have one foot in the classroom. "What? I don't know what you're talking about."

He rolls his eyes. "Remember the other night we were at the library and you had to leave? I sent you the link about the big mystery."

Oh. That.

I throw my backpack on the desk and search for my phone. When I retrieve his message, I hold the phone up. "Found it. Sorry, it's been crazier than usual." I scroll through the message and hit the link. In a few seconds the page comes up. A realty listing.

I thrust the phone toward him. "What's this?"

His eyes light up. "There's a building for sale that's exactly what I'm thinking of for my salon. I wanted to show everyone and get their thoughts. See what you think."

The screen is so small it's hard to see the details. "What did the girls say?"

Daniel moves his chair closer. "They want to see it with me and my Dad. He said even though I'm not licensed yet if it truly is the perfect building, he'll buy it now. Wanna join us?"

"When?"

"This weekend."

I shake my head. "I would love to see it, really. It's Jenna's wedding. I'm in it. And Noah's upset about his girlfriend breaking up with him, and I promised I'd pick up Betty for the wedding and..."

Daniel raises his hands. "Whoa, Carla. Slow down. Are you okay?"

The drumbeat in my head seems louder than his voice. My vision narrows to the point that I succumb to darkness.

⧗⧗⧗

It takes a few blinks before I fully open my eyes, and then a few seconds before I realize a crowd surrounds me, looking down, as I'm sprawled on the floor. I sit up, trying to get my bearings.

Daniel speaks first. "Are you okay?"

He looks pale. The way they are staring at me, I probably do, too.

Rose kneels down so we're eye level. "Carla, we called the paramedics. You passed out."

I try to rise, but between weakness and Daniel's hands on my shoulders, I remain sitting up on the floor. "I'll be okay."

Sandy folds her arms and shakes her head, looking more like a security guard. "We'll decide that. You dropped like a sack of potatoes."

Daniel nods. "You have a lot going on. It's a good idea to get checked out. Stay seated and put your head between your knees. You need to get the blood flowing."

With a sigh, I resign myself to staying put. Then it hits me, they called the paramedics.

The way things are going, Wayne will be on duty and in the area, called to be my rescuer.

⧗⧗⧗

Fifteen minutes later with sirens blaring, Wayne and Nathan push through the doors with their gear.

Wayne pauses as soon as he sees me on the floor. "Carla?"

I do my best to smile. "Hey. It's nothing serious. I passed out. I'm sure it's stress."

Nathan puts the blood pressure cuff on me and starts pumping. "Let us be the judge of that."

Wayne kneels and flashes a light in my eyes. "Is it Noah? School?"

I shake my head. "It's very busy right now, especially with the wedding this weekend. I'm commuting every day. My body was just letting me know it's time to slow down. Somehow." I chuckle.

Claire's standing behind Wayne. "Is she okay?"

I look around and see Rose, Mitzi, Sandy, and Claire in a circle, surrounding us. Where's Daniel?

Nathan reaches for a walkie-talkie. "Carla, I have to ask. Are you pregnant?"

My laughter echoes throughout the hall. "That's a strong no."

Wayne clears his throat. "Okay. When did you last eat?"

I bite my lip as I try to think back. I didn't have breakfast. I don't remember grabbing dinner. When did I have a meal? "I don't remember. My stomach would growl and then I'd get busy and do the next thing."

Wayne shuts the medical bag. "It's probably hunger and low blood sugar, but you should be checked out at the ER to rule anything more serious out."

I start to open my mouth, but Wayne keeps talking. "You want to be well for the weekend, and for Noah. Please let us take you to the ER."

I look around and every head is nodding. "Okay. I'll go."

⧗⧗⧗

Nearly two hours later, Dr. Garrett returns his stethoscope to his neck and smiles. "The paramedics were correct, a Vasovagal episode most likely brought on by exhaustion. Your ECG and blood work were normal. Make sure you receive enough fluid intake and don't skip meals. It's important you have eight hours of sleep each night. I'd like you to go home and rest today. If you have any re-occurrence of symptoms, make sure you call the number on your paperwork."

Thank God the news isn't worse. "I have a senior citizen friend back home who loves to tell me that 'this too shall pass.' I'm in a wedding this weekend. School is over in October. Things will slow down. Eventually."

He writes a few things in the chart and excuses himself for a moment, returning with juice and graham crackers. "Carry snacks in your purse. Put reminders in your phone calendar for the simplest things like going to bed or giving yourself a fifteen-minute break. Little things can make a big difference."

I nod, but he's back to writing again.

"Okay. I'm done here. The nurse will be in soon with your discharge papers. I think Daniel followed the paramedic SUV so that you have someone to drive you back to the school. Consider taking it easy for the rest of the day."

"Thanks, Doctor. I will."

Another ten-minute wait and the nurse sets me up with instructions and papers to sign. Once I'm able to leave, I reach for my purse and leave the room. I'm not sure where Daniel is but I figure the lobby is a good place to start looking. When I push through the double doors, the first face I see is Wayne's. He's leaning up against the registration desk.

He looks up. "Hey. Feeling any better?"

"I am. You and Nathan were right. Please don't tell anyone back home. I don't want Noah or Jenna to worry."

"No problem, I'm not allowed to anyway. Remember? I'm just signing off on another transport. Did you need a ride or anything? We're heading back to Speculator Falls soon."

I glance around wondering how I could lose Daniel in such a small hospital. "I think Daniel is taking me back to school. That's where my car is. I'll figure the rest out."

He grins. "You always do."

Daniel's voice interrupts before I can respond as he jogs over from another lobby. "You're out. Sorry, I was chatting with Dad and lost track of time. He said you'll be okay if you listen to directions."

He nudges me with his elbow and both he and Wayne break into laughter.

That's when another familiar voice joins the conversation.

Will runs toward me, nearly skidding to a stop when he sees me flanked by Wayne and Daniel. "Carla?"

Chapter Thirty-Two

The moment I see Will, my throat dries. I try to say his name, but nothing comes out. I want to explain why the two men are once again at the hospital with me, and he's the one I'm happy to see. The constant machine beeps from other nearby patients doesn't help my headache.

Will extends a hand to my shoulder. "Are you okay? Daniel called me from your phone at the school and told me what happened. I got here as soon as I could."

I turn to Daniel, who winks, and I return my attention to Will. With a cough, I find my voice. "I fainted. It's been kind of crazy lately. The doctor said exhaustion." I look over to the two, who stand there, watching us. "Wayne's here for work, and Daniel followed the ambulance to make sure I had a way back to school. You, know, because my car is there. I'm definitely not ready to return to class."

Will's gaze remains on me. His response is nowhere near the last time we were at the hospital. "I could take you home if you want. It would give you time to rest." He drops his arm to his side.

"What about my car and getting to school tomorrow? My plan was to go in the morning and then head back to Speculator Falls in the afternoon to get ready for the wedding rehearsal."

Wayne fishes his keys out of his pocket. "My shift is over. Nathan and I have our cars in Speculator Falls. We have to drive the SUV back to the health care center back home. I can drive your car to your house and Nathan can follow. We'll get your vehicle back to you later tonight."

All the logistics hurt my head, but I realize one thing. Everyone's getting along.

Will gives Wayne a pat on the back. "If it's okay with Carla, that sounds like a great plan."

My smile feels weak, but my heart fills with excitement. "Thanks, everyone. Daniel, thanks for calling Will and making sure I was okay."

Daniel waves me off. "No problem, it's what friends do. Don't be in a hurry to come back. I'll share my notes with you, so go, and enjoy the wedding." He gives me a quick hug and exits.

Will places his hand on the small of my back, and his touch feels as if it has sparks attached. "Ready? Let's get you home."

☒☒☒

It's hard to pin just one emotion in the atmosphere in Will's truck as he helps me get settled and starts for Speculator Falls. It's not tension. We've been down that road before. This feeling, tinged with awkwardness, is ripe with hope.

My gaze rests on his strong jawline as he maneuvers the light traffic on the highway. "Thanks again for traveling here to check on me. It means a lot."

Will flashes a grin before returning his concentration to the road. "That call scared me. I guess I had to make sure you really were okay." He brushes the corner of his eye. A tear, perhaps? "You have good friends. I'm glad Daniel called."

"Did you tell anyone? I don't want anyone to worry. Especially Noah."

Will shakes his head. "As soon as I disconnected the call, I grabbed my keys and started for Gloversville. I'm sure it's lunchtime at school and Noah's brooding over Brittany."

"Yes, that. Another thank you I owe you. I appreciate you taking the time to talk to him. You have a consistent Godly perspective Noah needs." That I need, too.

"He's a great kid. Give it a week and Brittany will be a faded memory." Will taps the steering wheel. A nervous laugh escapes. "You'll probably think this is corny, but I want you to know you're an amazing mom. We never really had a chance to talk those weekends you came home, but I was exhausted trying to do half of what I know you accomplished every day."

"You're sweet. Thanks for saying that. I underestimated how hard school would be, particularly juggling it with my son's needs and the wedding. It's probably why I passed out."

He keeps drumming the wheel with his thumbs. "I want to say something else."

My breath catches. I grip the seat to prepare for what's next.

"You aren't a faded memory to me, Carla. I can't stop thinking about you."

My bottom lip starts to quiver and it takes a couple seconds to compose myself. "Will." I can barely eke out a whisper. "I feel the same way."

Will makes an abrupt turn into a parking lot, and pulls into a spot, letting the engine idle. He faces me. "I know our breakup hasn't been long, but a lot has changed."

I nod, feeling the tears dripping down my face. "I'm not the woman who can't make a decision anymore. It's always been you. I'm sorry it took me so long to realize that."

He reaches for my hand and caresses it. "We both made mistakes. I also think we've grown from them."

I intertwine my fingers with his and move as close as I can with the gearshift in the way. "I love you. You deserve to hear that every day."

Will leans in. "I love you. I love Noah." He chuckles when I let out a sob. "And I'm going to kiss you."

Our embrace carries enough heat to melt an igloo. When we separate, he places his hands on the gear and the wheel. "Wow. I think we'd better get back on the road. But where do we go from here?"

I pretend to fan myself. "Would you like to have dinner with Noah and me tonight?"

⧗⧗⧗

Will and I are watching a movie in my living room when we hear footsteps on the porch. The door opens and Noah waltzes in, throwing his backpack on the floor before heading toward us. He stops as soon as he sees us holding hands on the couch.

"Whoa. When did this happen? Why aren't you at school?"

"I needed some downtime before the wedding. God did the rest between Will and me. What do you think about us being back together?"

Noah plops on the couch and playfully hits Will on the shoulder. "It's all kinds of awesome."

The three of us order a pizza and finish the movie. Will even finds paper and a pencil to write out all that we have to do to prepare for Ben and Jenna's rehearsal and wedding. My stress dissipates as all his tasks and mine become ours.

Time for Will to leave, and we linger on the porch. He wastes no time wrapping his arms around my waist. The proximity no longer scares me. I circle my arms around his neck and enjoy more than one goodnight kiss.

"Thanks for dinner." He kisses me between each word.

"Thanks for staying."

"May I pick you up after I get out of work so we can do rehearsal things together?"

I open my eyes for a second and catch Noah lifting the shade, only to shake his head and close the blind. "You sure can. We make a great team."

He stuns me with one last knee-weakening kiss before hopping off the porch. "I'll see you tomorrow."

I put my hand on the door handle and turn to Will. "I love you."

Once he leaves, I return inside and find Noah wearing a lopsided grin.

"What?"

"You two looked like dorks out there."

I walk over to the couch and toss a pillow toward his head.

Noah catches it and sobers. "But I'm happy Will's back in our lives."

"Me too, bud." An idea pops to mind and I smile. "Let's pray it becomes permanent."

Chapter Thirty-Three

If there were a contest for happiest person in Speculator Falls, I'm not sure who would win. Ben looks like he's had Botox injections because his wide grin is frozen into place. Jenna's absolutely stunning during rehearsal walking down the aisle in jeans, a white t-shirt that the seniors at the center gave her that had "bride" stamped across the front, and a makeshift headpiece created from her bridal shower bows.

But then there's Will and me.

When we enter the church arm and arm, Jenna squeals and runs toward us for a hug. "I knew it! I knew you two would get back together."

Brooke walks over and also gives us a hug. "It's wonderful to see you two. I know you've been through a lot."

Will caresses my back. "We have. But we've learned a lot and our faith is stronger because of everything." He plants a kiss on the top of my head.

Ben reaches for something under the pew and then joins us. He thrusts some kind of can into Will's hand. "Here you go. You sure have some odd requests."

Will slaps Ben on the back. "It will make sense soon."

Pastor Craig calls us to gather up front and start the rehearsal. I can barely focus because my mind is on my agenda. I can't wait to sit with Will and Noah at the dinner, and for us to head back home. Every time I catch a glimpse of Noah, his smile is almost as wide as Ben's.

It's nearly eleven before Will pulls into my driveway. We all laughed and joked through the rehearsal, so it took twice as long. I'm still determined to see my idea through, despite the late hour.

I face Will as he puts the truck in park. "Did you want to come in for a little bit?"

He stifles a yawn and stretches. "We have a long day tomorrow, but I don't want to say goodbye just yet."

Noah exits the vehicle and is inside the house before I can unbuckle my seatbelt and find my purse on the floor.

Will chuckles. "He should run track."

We take our time walking to the porch. I reach for his hand, my own palms wet from nerves. "So, tomorrow Ben and Jenna finally marry."

He nods. "Been a long time coming."

"Sure has. Speaking of long time coming, I wanted to ask you something."

Will stops before we reach the bottom step and releases my hand. Not that I can blame him with my palms. "What's going on?"

I clear my throat. "Okay. Well, now that we're back together, I don't want to waste a minute. I spent too much time taking you for granted."

He doesn't speak, but Noah turns the porch light on and it illuminates Will's head into a golden halo.

I start to bend on one knee. "Will, I love you."

He shakes his head and raises his hands. "Wait, Carla. Don't."

I start to lose balance and confidence. Was he rejecting me before I could ask?

Noah throws open the door and steps out. "Here you go, Will."

My son hands something over to him. Suddenly I smell something fruity.

"What's going on? Noah, don't you have something to say? You know? Our plan?"

He shakes his head. "Nope." Laughter follows.

Will takes my hand and pulls me up.

I hold my hand up in protest. "Noah and I are supposed to ask you…"

Everything in my plan changes when Will drops to one knee. "Is it okay if I go first?"

My legs start to shake. "Y-yes."

"Like you said, I don't want to waste time. I love you and Noah so much. In fact, I went to him and asked if I had his blessing."

My entire body trembles.

His voice catches. "And he was gracious enough to give it. With that, Carla, will you marry me?"

I'm crying and shaking enough that I'm having trouble speaking, but my incessant nodding doesn't seem like enough.

Noah jumps off the porch. "She's saying yes!"

Will stands and takes my hand. "Since this is sudden, I don't have the ring you deserve. But I remember when you were sheriff visiting Jenna for lunch at the senior center, you'd eat the fruit cups that Jenna always made fun of."

A sticky, almost slimy circle slides down my ring finger.

I lift my hand and find my voice. "A pineapple ring? I love it." I wrap my arms around him, traces of pineapple hitting the back of his neck. Noah joins in, spreading his arms against both of us.

Noah's the first to say it. "I love you guys."

Will tousles Noah's hair, still in need of a trim, and then my fiancé leans in to give me a quick kiss. "You have no idea how much I love both of you."

Epilogue

It's rare in the Adirondacks to have all the car windows down in early April, but Will, Noah, his new friend from school, Alyssa, and I drive to Lake George feeling the sun's warmth on our arms and faces.

Alyssa has no trouble making conversation. "How long have you two been married?"

Will winks at me, most likely remembering our fireworks. "We got married on July Fourth."

She scrunches her eyebrows together. "But you only dated since May."

I nod. "The second time. We knew after that we were meant to be together forever."

Alyssa turns to Noah. "And you helped them both propose to each other."

He laughs. "Will kind of hijacked Mom's proposal. It all worked out."

"And now we're visiting a hair salon?"

The vehicle GPS chirps a new directive.

I nod. "Yes. The class I graduated with is opening a salon together later this year. The owner wants me to see how renovations are going."

That seems to satisfy the teen. She reaches for one of Noah's earbuds and places one in her ear, while he keeps the other.

Will follows the electronic directions until we reach the address Daniel provided. "Here we are."

I look at the awning and see the fancy lettering. *Sanctuary: Comprehensive Salon.*

Before we reach the French doors, a familiar face opens them for us.

"Betty?"

She nods and giggles. "Do you know how hard it was to keep this secret all these weeks when you'd call and ask how I was doing?"

We walk inside and I give her a hug.

Daniel's greeting breaks up our reunion. "You might have beaten me on the boards, but I was able to convince your former landlord to put her house for sale and move here to be my office manager."

I squeal and run over to him, accepting another hug. "If Betty's part of your venture, you definitely win any competition we have going between us. Thanks for inviting us. I can't wait to see everything."

Once I step back, Will stands by my side and shakes Daniel's hand. "This place looks amazing. Where's everyone else?"

Daniel looks upstairs. "Painting. Come on, let me show you around."

Will and I sprint up the stairs while Noah and Alyssa hang back with Betty. The fumes guide the way to the room where Mitzi, Sandy, and Claire all are in separate corners painting.

Daniel knocks on the one dry wall. "Look who's here."

The women look over.

"Carla!" Mitzi drops her brush and runs over. Sandy and Claire follow her.

Claire stands next to Daniel. "What do you think of our manicure and pedicure room?"

This is so much bigger than the modest house Will and I bought with a salon in the back.

"You guys are amazing. When do you plan on opening for business?"

They all exchange looks.

Sandy speaks first. "June."

Daniel's answer nearly intercepts hers. "Before Memorial Day."

With that, they walk us through the shampoo station, the stylist chairs, and hair color area. Claire shows off the facial and makeup area while Sandy introduces us to the coffee lounge.

Will folds his arms. "It looks like you thought of everything."

Daniel nods. "I dreamed of all of this. Now, enough about me. How are the newlyweds?"

I lean against Will. "No complaints."

Mitzi steps forward. "Is your salon open?"

Will massages my arm. "You wouldn't believe how busy she is. Carla's attracting clients from all over Hamilton County. I'm so proud of her."

Sandy turns on the cappuccino machine. "What's been your biggest challenge?"

I don't even have to think. "A three-year old curly red head received an impromptu haircut when her hair became one with a piece of hard candy. It was a tangled mess I didn't think I could ever fix."

I turn and smile at my husband. "But after a quick prayer, I was able to sort through the curls and pull most of the hair away from the candy."

The group laughs as I recall the battle of wits between the mother and daughter. "At first the poor thing denied there was anything wrong, but when I untangled the candy and the hair, she started to cry. She thought she'd have to live with that missing patch of hair forever as proof of her mistake. It was fun to end the session with a hug, letting her know that one choice wouldn't last forever. I gave her a piece of chocolate and she was on her way."

Claire inches closer to Daniel, reaching for his hand. "That is the cutest story."

Will bends down and kisses the top of my head. "That little girl reminds me of someone."

Finally, I can think about my past and smile. "True. And like her, I plan to move on from my mistakes, eat chocolate, and be on my way." I face my husband and wink. "Doing it all with you by my side.

If you loved Entangled...

It would mean a lot if you would leave a positive review on at least Amazon and Goodreads. It takes a couple minutes of your time and makes a world of difference. If you aren't sure what to write when leaving a review, include a couple standout moments you enjoyed without giving the plot away, and don't mention knowing the author. If a reader sees that a reviewer wrote that the author is a friend or something similar, the reader thinks the review isn't accurate.

Thank you!

I appreciate you reading ENTANGLED. If you're struggling with choices you've made in the past, I encourage you to go to Christ and ask for His forgiveness. He will grant it. That's all you need. Don't allow guilt or fear to rule you, walk in the freedom Christ went to the cross for.

Coming Soon:

Engaged: Surrendering the Future

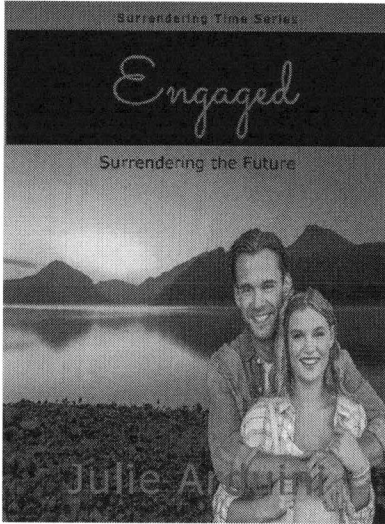

Trish Maxwell returns to Speculator Falls with crushed dreams, egg on her face, and the chance to make a new start with the very people and places she used to make fun of. She works hard and tries to convince the people of Speculator Falls she's not the princess she used to be.

As Trish pitches in with community events, she meets paramedic Wayne Peterson, the one man who doesn't seem to judge her. Living in New York City has always been her goal, but the more she's around Wayne and the Adirondack area, the more she's drawn to revising her plan.

Engaged

Chapter One

Shirley McIwain and her specs enter the Speculator Falls Department Store right before closing. Nothing like a big pair of bug-eye glasses to magnify my troubles. The right thing to do is greet her and see if she needs help. But, that's the issue, I'm only the help, the closer while mom attends a fancy lawyer meeting in Albany with Dad. Shirley's one of the senior citizens at the center I directed. The woman I handed the keys to in a cloud of dust when I left with no notice to start a new job in New York City. Can she smell my fear now that she's walking closer?

She saunters down the main aisle, stopping to pick up the black bear figurines and to sniff a vanilla candle. From there she walks up the slight slope that leads to the clothing section. Where the register is located. And where I'm pretending to read the weekly paper.

Please don't come over and ask me why I'm back in Speculator Falls.

As Shirley crosses the threshold and enters the world of sweatshirts, flannel and every kind of Adirondack logo imaginable, she stops near the gloves and picks up a pair, seeming to inspect them as she holds them up to the light. "Do you think you made a mistake?"

I look around and realize it's just us inside the store. I lean closer. "Excuse me?"

She returns the gloves to the stand. "You know, Trish Maxwell. A mistake."

I clear my throat and walk toward the woman with jet black hair curled under in a style that has to be older than me. "Is it the gloves? I sell the gloves. I don't make them."

Shirley rolls those big eyes of hers. "Not the gloves. You, Trish. You couldn't wait to leave Speculator Falls for the big city. When you left, the senior center shut down. Remember? Your ex-boyfriend? Poor councilman Ben Regan was so upset with no staff, and he didn't think as a volunteer it was appropriate for me to manage the center. Then there was the reminder of what you did to him, leaving the way you did. Ben made sure he closed the center for what he hoped would be forever."

A line of perspiration slides down my back.

She's not wrong. But talk to Shirley? No thanks.

"All so you could fulfill that dream of yours. But just like that, you returned."

I clench my hands together to control the sudden shakes.

"And in not much more than a year, city girl Trish Maxwell is back in Speculator Falls without a permanent job, helping her mom at the store."

I try to swallow, but my throat catches as the perspiration continues down my backside.

"So I wonder, was leaving here a mistake?"

My eyes start to roll and my knees give out.

⧗⧗⧗

"Trish? Can you hear me?"

A male voice, almost a whisper, is the first thing I hear before I even open my eyes.

But the person I see, close up, is Shirley hovering over me. Those big pupils can really scare a person.

"What's going on?" I try to sit up, but my head collides with Shirley's. A hand lands on my shoulder and presses me down to the floor.

"Trish, I need you to stay down until I've finished examining you. Shirley? Could you do me a favor and give us a little room?"

Shirley disappears, and kneeling before me is Wayne Peterson, Hamilton County paramedic. I didn't know his eyes were Caribbean blue.

"What happened?" Left on the floor, all I'm able to do is gaze into those ocean blues while he flashes a light between mine.

Wayne clicks off the light. "You fainted."

Shirley pipes up from across the room. "Remember? I was asking if you regret leaving the senior center and Speculator Falls for a job in New York that didn't even last a year. Your eyes got really big and then they rolled. Next thing I know, you're on the floor."

Right. The whole mistake question.

A whiff of breezy aftershave dances around my nostrils.

"Have you been sedentary today, Trish?" Wayne places his hand under my back and gently assists me to a sitting position.

I take a deep breath. "It's October in Speculator Falls. Not exactly turning the customers away here." I wave my hand to gesture but feel a stab across my forehead.

Wayne lays a hand to steady me. "Duly noted. What I mean is, did you move a little fast after a period of non-activity? I think your blood pressure dropped and your body reacted."

Ugh. Why didn't I stay behind the counter and let Shirley shop without help?

"Yeah, that sounds about right."

"I called for help right away. I even put the 'closed' sign on the door so no one would come in," Shirley said.

That basic First Aid class at the senior center apparently did my former assistant some good. "Thanks. I appreciate it."

Wayne velcroes the blood pressure cuff around me and pumps. When he finishes, he makes direct eye contact. "Everything looks good, but I want to take you to the primary care center and get you looked over. Although your floor is carpeted, you did fall, and I want to make sure you don't have a concussion." He gently pulls on my hand and helps me stand.

"I'll take her." Shirley waves her hand.

"No." I don't want to lose contact with my rescuer. "I mean, I need your help here. Ben's probably next door closing the store. I'm sure he'd help you close here, too."

Shirley looks to Wayne. "Did you bring the bus?"

He raises an eyebrow. "I'm sorry?"

"Ambulance. Can you take her to the medical center?"

Wayne grins and his five o'clock shadow looks completely adorable.

How have I missed him in this small village?

"Gotcha. Ms. McIwain, you watch too many cop shows. But, sure. I have the SUV. I'll transport her."

He winks and I sigh.

Shirley's incessant questions before I fainted come to mind. Mistake? Shirley has no idea.

⧗⧗⧗

The good news about fainting on the job is I did so near the end of the day. The Speculator Falls Primary Care Center's near vacant when Wayne brings me in. A girl walks out with a pink cast on her arm when the nurse calls my name.

"What brings you here this evening?" The woman looks to Wayne, not me.

"This is Jay Maxwell's daughter. She was at the department store when she passed out. I think it was a blood pressure drop."

She glances over at me. "The one who left the senior center for the city?"

So my reputation precedes me.

"And lost her job and is back." It's always fun to talk in third person.

"Well, Trish, let's see how you're doing. Wayne, you on duty?"

He looks to his watch and rakes his fingers through his messed brown hair. "Just off." He turns to me. "But I can wait and take you home."

I inhale, hoping to catch another whiff of that tantalizing cologne.

"Not like I've got anything else to do." Wayne turns on his heel and heads to the small waiting room.

Wayne must've learned tact from Shirley.

Thirty minutes later, the nurse throws open the curtain partition. "Dr. Augustine wants you to follow these instructions. Everything looks okay, including the x-ray, but he wants to make sure you guard against head injury and see your family doctor as soon as possible. Sign here and you're good to go."

I press on the clipboard as I scribble my name and hand the paperwork back to her.

Wayne stands as soon as he sees me. "All set?"

"Yes, thanks. I appreciate your help."

He doesn't guide me to the car, but he opens the passenger door for me, a gesture I haven't experienced since dating Ben Regan. "You live with your parents, right?"

I close my eyes. It sounds so awful to hear it out loud. "Yes."

"Good. That way you won't be alone in case you have any complications. Not that I think you will." He starts the SUV and puts it in drive.

"How about you, Wayne? You kind of arrived in town when I was away. Do you live alone?" Because I don't see a ring on his finger.

He turns onto Route 8. "Kind of."

I raise my eyebrows. "That's mysterious."

He chuckles, a low tone that's music to hear. "I don't mean to be cryptic. It's not a cut and dried answer. I live alone most of the time. However, I have a son. Sometimes he stays with me."

Although it's dark, I turn to look for a hint of laughter or sarcasm. There's none. "Oh. So, you're divorced?"

Another tenor laugh. "Is your name Shirley? You ask a lot of questions."

"Sorry. I don't have a lot of people to talk to these days." Not that I did when I lived here the first time.

"I hear ya. It can get pretty dull during most of my shifts, too. To answer your question, no. I'm not divorced. To head off the next question, never married."

Interesting.

"It's not glamorous, but I became a dad when I was a teen. And I know Shirley gave you some pressure about your choices. You can only imagine how my hometown felt about mine."

If his birthplace is as small as Speculator Falls, I'm sure the news spread from one end of the village to the other in five minutes.

"You probably know my son. He's with his mom and step-dad a lot. Noah Rowling-Peterson. Carla Marshall is his mom."

A flash of a young man with Carla and Will Marshall at church comes to mind. Seems like he had trouble not so long ago, but I can't recall more than that. "That's right."

"This your folk's house?" He points to the Maxwell abode, front porch light on just waiting for me to drag my sorry self inside.

He pulls in the driveway and puts the vehicle in park. "Try not to overdo it."

I open the door and hold up the papers. "I promise I'll follow the instructions."

"Okay. Well, it looks like you're going to be fine."

Until I face Shirley or any of the still furious senior citizens again.

"I think so. Have a good night." I climb out and wave.

I take three steps when I hear my name.

"You know, what Shirley said?"

"Yes?"

"I hope you don't think coming back to Speculator Falls is a mistake."

My laugh exposes my breath and nerves against the cold air.

ACKNOWLEDGEMENTS

They say the second book is the hardest, and ENTANGLED: Surrendering the Past was no exception.

My Prayer Covering team, you know who you are, your prayers rescued me from delay, discouragement, and detours.

My thanks to Scribes 202 and Scribes 210 for their critiques. You make writing look easy.

Kim Bilas, you were an answer to prayer with your editing. Julie Brown and Holly Hrywnak, thank you for being such faithful BETA readers.

April Heeter, thank you for letting me to take your cosmetology book and ask you all kinds of questions, and for being patient with my stubborn cowlick.

Pastor Gary Gray, thank you for permission to use notes from your sermons in my work.

Aiden Bailey, thanks for help with Noah's shirt. Carol Childers, thank you for giving me vision for Will Marshall.

The CIA (Christian Indie Author) Facebook group, thank you for the treasure trove of information. Elizabeth Maddrey for formatting help, and Tracie Corll for her bookmark help/listening to me whine.

Hannah Arduini, Tom Nuttall and the Entrusted book club ladies, thank you for the accountability. Tracy Ruckman, thank you for your grace. Alyssa, Amber, and the many teens I've encountered over the years, thank you for letting me hang out with you.

Mom, for supporting me in every possible way.

Crista, Landon, Mandy, Randy, Matt, Stephanie, and Nicole, for being great cheerleaders.

Tom, Brian, and Hannah, for grace as I pretty much lost my mind during the process and you kept spurring me on.

To the One who has forgiven me even when I go way past 70x7 with my sin, every word is for Your glory.

Made in the USA
Charleston, SC
13 January 2017